The Future Past of an Extraordinary Man

Memories of a time to come

The Autobiography of Luke Macdonald

b. 2003 -d. 2091

Imagined by Rob Clarke

eBook ISBN: 978-1-966931-31-7
Paperback ISBN: 978-1-966931-32-4
Hardback ISBN: 978-1-966931-33-1

This book is a work of fiction.

The foreseen extreme weather events are based on the scientific predictions at the time of writing.

The described animal agriculture processes are based on the government-approved standards of animal welfare.

All references to people currently alive are fictitious

1 October 2024

Contents

Dedication

To my wife Susan for her unrelenting campaigning for the recognition of all animals' right to a natural life.

About the Author

Rob Clarke is a successful businessman living in their family home in Southeast England with his wife, Susan. His study into how the future emerges from the present, a lifelong interest in politics and a love of storytelling have informed his debut novel.

Two years of scientific research have illuminated the probable consequences of human-induced climate change and the loss of habitat for the planet's dominant species, humankind. His solution is to allow the planet to heal itself before our species self-destructs. This novel is his human story cast into the future with wide-ranging predictions and an optimistic outcome.

Prelude

November 2091 Surrey, England

Another tropical storm clattered on the window of his 19th-century country house when Luke Macdonald, philanthropist, author, playboy, father and friend, finally accepted that tomorrow he will die.

The sparkle in his eyes was dulled by sadness, disappointment and fear. Luke had always believed that involuntary euthanasia at the biological age of 80 was the only way to manage the population, encourage healthier lifestyles and reduce the burden of old age on society. Today, he was not so sure. His time had come.

Exercise and diet had kept him alive well beyond his chronological age, but time has crept up on him. He will die on his 88th birthday, alongside some older and some younger. Made anonymous by old age and facing dying by enforced altruism, Luke would escape the hardships and embarrassments of natural expiry, but he now rushed to keep his memories alive before the darkness of death consumed him.

PART ONE

Danger

Of Man's first disobedience and the fruit

Of that forbidden tree whose mortal taste

Brought death into the World, and all our woe

With the loss of Eden

Paradise Lost

John Milton 1667 (Abridged)

Chapter 1

I woke with the piercing whistle from my alarm. The time, 6:30 am and the date, 27th November in the year 2091, screamed at me from the ceiling display. I didn't sleep well last night. Maybe it was the humid atmosphere, the failing air conditioning or the tropical storm. Perhaps I didn't sleep well because today, my eighty-eighth birthday, is to be my last day alive.

I showered awkwardly as my old body needed the wall support to maintain my balance. After two minutes under the ready-soaped water spray, the warming blasts of air dried my old skin before the mist of 111SKIN body lotion prepared me for the walk-through solarium that created my undeserved healthy appearance. A light cream removed my day-old stubble, and my LED screen whitened my teeth. I will die looking good. I decided to be happy.

My unsteady balance is a challenge as I struggle into my day clothes, a loose-fitting body stocking in dark blue that still clings to my fading muscles. I used to buy my attire from the best tailors, but now everything is delivered from the Sain Super Store. I chuckle to myself as, not for the first time, I reflect on how nice it would be to go in Sain.

I take the stairs carefully as I move downstairs to my study, a room lined with decaying books from the 20th Century. Soon, the stormy dark skies of night will roll back to reveal the clarity of daylight. I like the cool of November, but I detest the short days. It will be dark by 4:30 pm this afternoon. In my study, I can capture glimpses of the morning light through a twelve-paned Georgian window overlooking the tree-lined public right of way that strolls past my Surrey home. With my study door left open, I catch sight of an old man in the mirror in the adjoining hallway. His watery eyes, soft features and bushy grey hair surely can't be me. The man in the mirror can't be preparing for his own death.

I sit fidgeting in my chair until the November sunshine and blue skies break into the morning, splashing optimism into my pond of despair. Has my life been a waste of time? Have I just been another selfish consumer of the planet's scarce resources? I feel an urgent need to tell my story, to let the world know what really happened and to justify my existence. I have had a lifetime of being a listener, not a talker, an observer, not the observed, a spectator, not the actor, but now is the time to tell my story. With only 16 hours to do it, I will miss some things, offend friends, expose others and get some things wrong. Please forgive my errors.

I was born in 2003, at a time when the greedy population of the world would not accept that the planet's resources were limited. Economic growth and ever-increasing personal consumption were a target for all governments.

A more realistic ambition was just emerging, as extreme weather events justified the scientific warnings. I was too young to realise how this century would demand changes and how less aggressive ethics would emerge.

Real life for me started at university when I met Beth, but first, I must tell you how I got there and how my childhood formed my future. I have few memories of the early years, that time of innocence when we carry no hopes or fears, no ambitions and no prejudices, a time when we could be saints or sinners and not understand the difference. Innocence is too soon overtaken by knowledge, expectations by experience, and optimism by cynicism.

I do recollect 2007 and the birthday cake for my fourth birthday. Two unremembered companions from nursery school, together with my friend Josh and my first little sister, Amelia, sat round the kitchen table with my parents. Mum and Dad Macdonald were partners of contrast. My father was easygoing and too ready to please, whilst Mum was disappointed with life even after only a few short years of marriage. Baby sister Amelia chortled happily in the blue highchair that she had inherited from me.

Escaping red jelly and scattered unwanted crusts from the banana sandwiches smudged the white tablecloth. Shining young faces, splattered with jam from the tarts, looked up as the birthday cake arrived. The sponge cake stuffed with cream and decorated with white icing hosted four red candles.

A miniature football player stood in the middle of blue icing letters, spelling "Happy Birthday" to the uncomprehending children. The candles were lit into scaled-down flames by my father's proud hand. All I had to do was to make a wish and blow so that the tiny flames would disappear.

The candles wouldn't blow out. However hard I tried to blow, they burst back into life, to my embarrassment and everybody else's amusement. Nobody explained that they were trick candles. My mother, pretty in a yellow dress and a sparkling necklace that only appeared for special occasions, laughed too, placing her need to conform before her awareness of my acute embarrassment. Father comforted me and helped me hide my tears as I learned not to show my vulnerability. His concern when everybody else was laughing would be something that I have recalled often in future years. Back then, I thought that this failure to blow out the lucky candles whilst I was making a wish would bring bad luck for my whole life, and perhaps it did.

The memory of that pain haunts me even now. I blamed the unresponsive candles when I didn't get the puppy I'd prayed for, or later the red bicycle, or when I had to wear braces on my teeth, even when Arsenal beat Chelsea in the Cup Final and, amazingly, when I was first teamed up with Bess. There would be many more opportunities for me to curse my luck and blame the candles.

My second sister, Freya, was born before my fifth birthday and I became unnoticed in a family overwhelmed by the needs of two babies whilst my father was starting a new career in the railways. I learned to watch and listen. Staying quiet was the only option as my sisters grew older and bonded like twins.

As four years too quickly became fourteen, I pretended an insecure confidence. I was taller than my peers and had a face that people liked, not conventionally handsome but open and, it seemed, agreeable. I used this unearned advantage to the full, drawing in friendships, avoiding punishment for unintentional misdemeanors and influencing friends and family. I worked hard for exams but pretended to be casual about revision. Although never brilliant, I always enjoyed good grades. A close friendship with the more bookish Josh gave us both support and together, we knew no fear. The only sport I excelled in was sprinting. My school record of 11.1 seconds for the one hundred metres stood until I left school. Maybe it's still the record if the school still exists. I had inherited my father's easy-going readiness to please and his unwillingness to display his own feelings for fear of upsetting others and, as a result, I was well-liked. Each day, I decided to be happy. My unexpected popularity encouraged a self-assurance that hid my certain knowledge that my ideas did not deserve the credibility afforded by others.

I was an ordinary teenager with conflicted beliefs a desire to change the world but no idea how to approach the challenge. I had learnt how to hide my insecurity and began to think that I would do something special with my life. In that, I ask you, my readers, to be judge.

Chapter 2

Here comes Peter, my personal assistant and carer, with my breakfast. He doesn't say much and his quiet stare gives him a disapproving appearance that I find disquieting. I do need his care and he seldom, if ever, complains about my grumpiness. He looks smart this morning in his crisp white linen overall, which seems to be his winter uniform.

I can't see much point in a healthy breakfast or any food at all, but I will eat to show Peter that all is normal. The seeds and nuts, with oranges from the garden, look quite tasty. What would Peter say if he knew what I was dictating and that I would immortalise him in my memoir. What would he do in his final hours? He is still quite young. At his age, I would have wanted to spend my last hours with at least two beautiful naked girls in a spacious bed. Now I realise how futile that experience would be for my last day, even if I had the energy for it.

By the time I was 14, my brain had slipped down below my torso and all I thought about was girls. My lively imagination was fuelled by soft pornography on my computer tablet and iPhone and the bragging of my school friends. I had no hands-on experience with girls when I attempted my first kiss.

At secondary school, I had formed a contemporary pop group with Josh and his sister Emily. Josh was shorter than my gangly frame and his spectacles gave him an intelligent look that foretold his ability. He always looked serious and acted like a straight man as we joked our way through school. Somehow, his honest vulnerability made him popular, although I could never fathom why. Josh played guitar and claimed to have mastered the fingering through lessons on an acoustic instrument at school.

With this limited knowledge he made his own sounds with an electric guitar. His elder sister, Emily, was a good singer and was hot. I played an electric organ with more gusto than style. Hated piano lessons had left me with enough knowledge to make a sound rhythm, but little space for the melody. I thought that I was going to be a pop star. Our first performance was at a school dance where Josh and I spent the whole time trying to impress any admiring girl fan. We had no success. All our friends and school mates ogled Emily. To my surprise, we were then asked to perform at an adult garden party, a real gig for money.

When the day came, I spent hours gelling my hair, shining my teeth and admiring myself in the white tracksuit bottoms and a bright yellow tee shirt I had selected from my limited wardrobe. I hoped that nobody would notice my tired, dirty white trainers. I can't remember Josh's stage outfit except that his pocket bulged with an eating apple he had sneaked out of his house. I couldn't forget Emily's outfit. She wore a short, sparkly mini dress, bought with the money she had earned from her Saturday job at New Look. She was almost boy-like with her slight figure and close-cropped hair. She looked a million dollars, the centre of attention, on the small stage, in the open air, her short dress reflecting her summer skin. Performing gave me an adrenalin kick. When the audience danced to the rhythm I felt in control of the thirty or so adults who took to the floor. After the performance, I returned to the empty house and to the bedroom we were using as a changing room. Josh was nowhere to be seen. I guess that he was quietly eating the apple.

Emily was in the room, lying on the rumpled bed, exhausted by her performance. She was looking fabulous with her rumpled skirt swishing around her sunburnt thighs. As she stood up from the bed, I grabbed her rather roughly and bent forward, forcing the kiss I had dreamt about firmly against her protesting mouth. Emily screamed as though in pain and pushed me away, saying, "Go away, stupid child!" She was much older than me, nearly sixteen, I think.

For the first time, I was frightened by what I had done. Would Emily tell? What would she say? Was I in trouble? Was it a sexual assault? Was I a rapist? I felt exposed and confused about what I had done. Not knowing what else to do, I returned to the party. I hid my embarrassment behind the allowed cola. Emily ignored me. Josh didn't say anything, either. I tried to put the whole experience to the back of my mind, blaming the childhood birthday candles. Feeling alone and disgusted with myself, I quickly left the party.

I never told anyone. For months, I lived in fear that this aggressive behaviour would be exposed. I never gigged again. I didn't try to kiss another girl for four years, but then Bess was very different.

Chapter 3

Childish worry is so intense. Re-living the fear I felt when I was fourteen has brought tears to these watery old eyes. I sit here wondering how my life would have been changed if Emily had complained. I later learned that an event so significant to me was soon forgotten by Emily, but that's a story for later. There are many crossroads in a lifetime, and lots of opportunities for disaster to strike and time and again, I wonder how I escaped the calamity.

If I don't hurry along, I will never reach the end of my tale. Let me tell you about my university time. As a lustful but nervous eighteen-year-old student, I expected university to be one of the best times of my life. In the end, it was. It was my introduction to girls and to politics. It would also show me both kindness and cruelty. It was a tricky start to my adult life.

My education had been disrupted by the COVID lockdowns in the previous year, but generous marking of A Level exams helped me and Josh gain places at Exeter University. Josh to read Environmental Science because he had set his sights on a job at the Met Office. He wanted to be a television weather forecaster. In the end, he was much more successful as a climatologist in space exploration. I chose Politics and International Relations because I really had no plan for my future.

At first, university life was restricted by COVID. The pandemic had started in Wuhan, China, probably because of the mishandling of infected farmed animals. Over three million people have lost their lives as a result and many more are disabled by long COVID. At the time I never thought about how or why or the possibility of its return. I was only interested in beer, girls and how to attract them.

Although Josh and I lived in different Halls, we got together at least twice a week. I expected that my schoolboy popularity would transmit to university but now I found myself uncertain and tongue-tied, especially when talking to girls. My pleasant features and willingness to please were no longer sufficient to attract female students who were seeking fun, wit or intelligent conversation, all of which were beyond my limited ability.

When Josh and I weren't out partying and trying, usually unsuccessfully, to attract girlfriends, we did discuss the impending climate emergency and UK politics over a beer or two at the Victoria Inn. The pub was a depressing building on a quiet suburban corner, but inside, under low beamed ceilings, it was always crowded by students chasing heavy pints of gassy local beer with cheap shots.

The arguments got stronger and the noise louder as each round of drinks gave the students the confidence to enhance their reasoning. Nobody realised that saying the same words, but louder, does not make them more convincing. Discussions were often brushed away in the swirling sea of student dialogue and impossible discourse on meaningless debate. Only a few students were worried about the impending climate change. Their ambition to free society of carbon fuels mirrored popular beliefs.

Students formed groups of activists, mainly vegan girls I didn't fancy. Other than Josh, none of my friends had the foresight to do much about the impact on the climate of our lifestyle and food choices. Josh wouldn't use a petrol car, had adopted a plant-based diet that often was just an apple, cycled everywhere and wore the same jeans and t-shirt for every occasion to avoid polluting washing powders. His lifestyle choices and the ever-present aroma of his armpits did inhibit his courtships. He said, "Activism is essential and anything else would be giving up on humanity." He campaigned against waste and over consumption every weekend to create awareness and political change, but all to no avail.

Poor old Josh has passed now. His funeral was attended by over 200 people who spoke so highly of his kindness and his contribution to technology. Josh would have been amazed. I so miss his presence and his bumbling lack of self-regard. He knew me better than most, could see through my uncertainty and was a true friend. His wife, Ava, told me that she had slipped an apple in his casket to make sure he wasn't hungry on his onward journey. That would have made him laugh.

Nobody could dislike Josh. His simple dress sense and

personal modesty hid an immense brain in which so many ideas competed for his attention. He was sometimes totally assured, sometimes uncertain, as the contradictory scientific "facts" that flew from his tablet were amplified by his enthusiasm. The activists became his friendship group and they all agreed that something had to be done to protect the future of our species. They couldn't accept that so little was planned by the governments around the world. I couldn't believe that authorities would only watch as our own habitat was being destroyed. I hoped that they knew something that I didn't understand.

Like most of my fellow students, I thought that better brains than mine would sort it out and that technology would come to our aid in the end. I was more worried about getting a girlfriend, a good degree and a job. My consumption of the earth's resources was restricted by the limits of a student loan. I bought few clothes and only essential food, as drinks were awarded a higher priority in my budget. We worry about the wrong things when we are young, as I was to discover.

After halls in my first year, I shared my rooms with Josh and two students from the Faculty of Health and Life Sciences. Josh and I were returning there from the Victoria Inn when we were attacked. It had been an ordinary night in the pub, although I may have been over-garrulous and under-convincing in my defence of Animal Rising, a group of activists that were recruiting in Exeter. With the Dutch courage bestowed by three pints of Otter Ale, I intervened when we approached a group of boys surrounding, pushing and ridiculing two young girls because they were holding hands. I can't remember what I said to invoke such anger and violence, but I finished up in hospital with knife wounds.

An undeserving Josh, with a bruised face and body, sat alongside me, waiting to know that I would recover. It was from Josh that I learned how a knife had been pulled and I had taunted the holder with my contemptuous sneers until he plunged the weapon into my chest.

Josh had made a brave, if foolhardy, attempt to restrain the attacker but quickly took the opportunity for a hasty retreat, hauling me away from the action. A bystander had called the ambulance and I was blue-lighted to The Royal Devon and Exeter Hospital. I was beginning to realise that I was a fool beneath the cloak of confidence. The attacker, identified as most likely suspect by the police, was never charged. My birthday candles had struck again, but once more, I had survived, perhaps a little wiser.

I wasn't in hospital for long, but it was time for me to discover a novel love for classical music. Noticing my shaking head to the beat as I listened to Miley Cyrus singing "Flowers" in my headphones, a fellow patient persuaded me to try Mozart's Piano Concerto No. 23. I was immediately enraptured by the sounds that streamed directly into my brain; giving moments of gentle rest and contemplation interrupted with the most joyous of melodies. It took me months to put aside the many delights of his compositions and try the more complex sounds of Beethoven, Vivaldi and Bach always to return to the soulful optimism of Mozart. Maybe it is through 18th-century music that I learned how the passage of time does little to change mankind.

My second year was just ending when I met Bess Hurley. She was a vegan activist friend of Josh, with sturdy legs and an argumentative spirit. After all these years, I can't really remember what she looked like then, but even now, I feel a tingle when I think of her touch and our time together.

Prime Minister Rishi Sunack surprised political pundits when he called an election in July 2024, some months before it became obligatory. His party was well behind in the polls. Despite dire warnings from Josh that the Conservative party was paying scant regard to the climate emergency, I supported Rishi Sunak in his attempt to be elected against all odds. Of course, it was a bit about him being the underdog, but I felt that he was a safer bet than the unconvincing Labour alternative.

Sunak was a small man with an expensively pressed appearance and trousers that never quite reached his ankles. This indicated a serious mind that lacked imagination or adventure. His boring ambition was the antidote to the recklessness of his predecessors, Liz Truss and Boris Johnson. The new Conservative candidate for Exeter was a young, charismatic woman who had completed the same Exeter University course as I was studying only ten years ago. Tall, slim and angular, Brenda Limes was only thirty-one but, dressed in high-heeled shoes and a pencil skirt, she portrayed a no-nonsense approach that was a bit scary. Her job as a political researcher in the Home Office and having family in the area had helped her selection. Not expected to win this time, Brenda Limes was earning her right to be selected for a safer seat.

Josh went off to join the hopeless campaign for the Green Party. I joined the Conservatives and started door-to-door campaigning on behalf of Brenda Limes. She had feigned interest in me, and, for a while, I wondered if my enthusiastic appearance and earnest campaigning would earn me a place in her bed one night. My willingness to please was an inadequate gesture for that to become a reality.

I was teamed up with Bess, the vegan activist. I didn't want to listen to her endless campaign jargon. She felt an obligation to instruct me in the horrors of animal agriculture and its threat to the planet. Bess was irritating. My candles were still delivering their witchcraft.

Together, Bess and I went out every evening for five weeks, knocking on doors, posting leaflets and delivering our message that the Conservatives "Have a Plan" and stood for "Integrity, professionalism and compassion." Conservatives would get the job done. This simple message had absolutely no evidence to support it but despite the Conservative record in power, the mantra seemed to satisfy most neighbours in the better parts of the city without alarming residents in the poorer areas. In those days an election required the completion of a written vote and then the counting of slips of paper as each named a single candidate. The candidate with the most votes was elected and the minority votes counted for nothing.

My annoying canvassing partner, Bess, was a pretty girl, tall if a little plump, not flattered by her stretched jeans and regular trainers. Her ready smile and dedicated commitment made walking around the demoralising streets just bearable despite her irritating need to instruct me on the cruelty of eating meat. On election day, we were allocated to the new Polling Station at the Church Hall for St Thomas the Apostle Anglican Church on Cowley Street. Inside, the hall had been transformed into reception and proof of identity areas and private voting booths where votes were cast. Election Day started with pleasant sunny weather but tiring heat gathered during the day.

From early morning, Bess and I sat outside the Church Hall entrance on borrowed picnic chairs, trying to tick off the names of the voters as they appeared. Any residents that were expected to be Conservative supporters who hadn't voted would be contacted and encouraged to cast their vote preference before the polling station closed at 10:00 pm.

As we sat by the red brick medieval church building, Bess did seem more attractive in a dress for the first time. Her ready smile helped her engage so easily with voters. I felt proud of her and flattered that we were seen as a couple together. Now that our campaigning tasks were behind us, Bess became an attractive woman, not the annoying campaigner for animal rights. That evening, when voting was over and the Polling Station closed, Bess and I were invited to the count at the Riverside Leisure Centre.

The sports hall had been transformed for the count. Council officials, enlisted for the night, scurried about between tables laden with voting slips, receiving sealed boxes, recording, distributing and counting the democratic wishes of the people of Exeter in an outdated method that had served the community well since 1872. Bess's appearance was transformed by her fashionable shoes and a simple dress that revealed her curvaceous figure and directed attention to the newly released blonde hair tumbling to her shoulders, her perfect smile and her clear complexion. We endured a long, nervous wait with fellow campaigners before the results were declared at 4:30 am. The Labour candidate had retained his seat but with a reduced majority of 5431.

Josh cheered the Green Party's surprise third place. The vote in Exeter had reversed the trend in the UK and surprised the pundits. We listened to the results across the country through the night and late into the morning. The UK voter turnout of only 52% was one of the lowest ever recorded.

The Labour Party enjoyed a landslide victory, albeit without an increase in the national vote. Keir Starmer had capitalised on the unpopularity of the Conservative government and inherited the difficult economic situation left by his predecessors.

Excited by the event, I had a happy, if tired, spring in my step as I left the hall with Bess. Outside the counting room, we walked into the torrential rain of a tropical storm. Perhaps I should have given more regard to Josh's warnings of climate change, but for now, I just wondered how I would get Bess home in her summer dress at 5:00 am in the morning.

In the end, I said, "Come to mine, it's just round the corner," and she didn't hesitate. We chased each other across glistening empty streets, clattering into oily puddles until we clambered up a jaded staircase to my first-floor shared flat. Whispering to avoid waking my snoring flat-share companions, I showed Bess to my cluttered bedsit. With her wet dress off but damp bra and pants intact, Bess slipped next to me into my wide bed and, with my mind still excited by the election results, we both fell into a deep and easy sleep.

The sunshine streaming through the thin curtains and dirty windows woke me late the next morning. A beautiful blue sky and bright sunshine had followed last night's thunderstorms. It did not, however, get my attention. My first morning view was of Bess studying my face with her eyes sparkling with kindness and affection. Without a word she turned and kissed me, at first gently and then with passion. I was only too ready to return her affection. I soon felt a desire that made me feel more alive than ever before. I found an undiscovered longing. As the sunlight steamed through the window, we made love slowly and lovingly. The taste and smell of Bess and my control over her desire brought every nerve in my body to the surface.

Memories of that day never leave me. I can still feel that release of passion and the comfort of her female body. I can taste and smell the newly made coffee and slightly burnt toast that followed our lovemaking. I remember the giggles as we chopped a wizened orange to replace the missing marmalade and the intimacy as we explored each other's bodies. We discussed what made us happy, where to kiss, stroke or cuddle, both of us unashamed of our naivety. Innocence is soon overtaken by experience, simplicity by complication, optimism by pessimism. Our joy in each other would not last.

Nobody seeing me now could imagine the strength of my desire almost seventy years ago. My love affair with Bess lasted the whole of the summer and through my final year at university. We both had summer jobs, mine at Moss Bros. I can't remember what Bess did. We spent most nights together, usually in her room. Bess had a pretty room in a house share in Park Road. With seven girls all sharing one bathroom, I wondered how they managed in term time, but, in the vacation, Bess and I usually had the house all to ourselves. The bedroom was, if not exactly tidy, a lot cleaner than mine.

All I really remember is counting the cracks in the ceiling as we lay in bed together, pondering the future. All our friends had gone home, but we only wanted each other. We could lay together in silence, listening to the Mozart's symphonies I had introduced to her and letting the music shape our bodies. We learned to dance together to the beat of Rufus Du Sol and Ellie Goulding. We walked the high Tors on Dartmoor, ran along the beaches at Blackpool Sands and planned our super yacht in the Torquay harbour. Bess appeared to be a shy girl, nervous about creating the wrong impression and fearful of being laughed at, but in private, she was wild. She was studying languages at Exeter and could swear in eight different British dialects, although none would fully hide her own northern tones. She could mimic her tutors and had a wealth of not-very-ladylike jokes learnt from her brothers. When Bess told a joke, she recounted it under constant giggles as she remembered the punchline before she reached it. Bess also had a passion that was so in contrast to my calculated attitude to life. Her zealous demand to end factory farming came directly from her soul. I admired the intensity of her love for all animals, including me. She put aside her activism for me but insisted that I never ate meat, fish or dairy products when we were together. I seldom did when we were apart.

Beth's indulgence was her nighttime bath as she took advantage of the empty shared house. She was often soaking for an hour before coming to bed carrying the sweet smell of her shampoo. The cleanliness of her body and the warmth of her skin carried a promise that I found irresistible.

Sex never became boring. We experimented with ideas we had seen on Porn Hub, but nothing matched the pure pleasure of simple lovemaking. We often tried outside in hidden corners or amongst the parkland flowers, where nature and the prospect of perhaps being watched added an extra dimension. I felt that I had become a man. My body had taken shape and my limbs, once skinny and uncertain like a newborn foal, had become powerful and, at last, coordinated and controlled. I was proud of how I was feeling, enjoying the tension of sexual expectation. I was thrilled by the impact I had on Bess, whose soft breasts, flat stomach and ample bottom I still remember.

It was another 39 years before I would discover just how big an impact these short months would have on my life.

Chapter 4

Peter has taken away my empty breakfast plates and gone to clean my bedroom and make my bed with cleanly pressed bed linen. It will be my final resting place. I already need a break from telling my story. A walk in the garden will help clear my head. This is my piece of England. This garden has sustained me now for 20 years with new growth that surprises me every spring and its spent debris every Autumn. Now that my eyesight is fading and I quickly get breathless, I still enjoy the smells of the garden, the jasmine that has its second flowering in November and the ever-present gardenia.

Mostly, the lavender along each side of the pathway has taken so much nurturing over the years but now creates smells that bring back so many memories of happy times. After the brown of the hot summer months, the grass is now green again and last night's rain will have left a dampness that reminds me of Lords Cricket Ground's lush outfield. I want to take my mind away from how I will miss the beauty that nature and I have nurtured here in Surrey. Thinking about cricket might help.

I remember the first time my father took me to a Test match. He invited Josh along as well. We both played cricket at school for the Under 15 eleven. Josh was a rather erratic fast bowler, with a run up almost as long as the school cricket field. I thought myself as a swashbuckling opening bat but had little success.

England were playing Australia at Lords in the second test match of a five-game series. It was a warm day in northwest London, with sunshine escaping the cloud cover in short bursts. I can't help but smile when I think of Josh, munching away on an apple as his vacant stare behind giant spectacles hid his concentration on the game. The gentle murmur of the spectators, only interrupted by enthusiastic cheers of appreciation from time to time, created a harmonious, friendly atmosphere.

The amiable banter elicited laughter that rippled around the stand. I was entranced by the contradiction of concentration and drowsing that distinguished fellow spectators. A kind ambiance underscored the collective experience. As a newcomer but not an outsider, I had found my family. The contest had me hooked as a cricket fan for the rest of my life. I loved sitting with 30,000 other cricket spectators, second-guessing the field placements and encouraging the nearby fielders. I listened to the raucous banter from the barmy army of vociferous fans and clapped enthusiastically at a gentle pace with the MCC members.

I visited Lords more recently, where little had changed except a more consistent summer sunshine. Cricket has been played in England since 1550. The sport's gentle reputation and intelligent strategies hide a fierce and dangerous competitiveness that characterises the English nature. Its continuity is reassuring. Surely, cricket will still be played in England in another four hundred- and fifty years' time.

Maybe cricket reflects my nature: clean and tidy like cricket whites, accepting rules, a simple contest between batter and bowler with hidden strategies for those who look deeper, competition masked by politeness. Cricket is played by a team of individuals where individual glory is as important as team victory and with a readiness to congratulate a worthy opponent.

My life has gone full circle. Since my first visit to Lords more than 70 years ago, so much has changed in the world and yet so little. Despite the many major changes, there is more the same in our lives than is different. Every over has six balls. There are winners and losers. The music of Mozart and the plays of Shakespeare are still performed on instruments that would have been recognised 250 years ago. Men and women sit around their meal tables discussing politics, complaining about their leaders and gossiping about their neighbours as they have done for centuries.

Chapter 5

With my life so nearly finished, what history do I leave behind? Will anybody be here for my last goodbye? I must tell my story and time is escaping my grasp. If I don't hurry, I won't get it all recorded before I must take the dreaded final pill. Taking your own medicine suddenly takes on a new meaning. I don't want to be alone when I take the final step, but nobody has offered their companionship. Will I only have the disapproving Peter at my side, avoiding any emotional connection? How will this recorded manuscript find the light of day once I face perpetual darkness? I feel all alone, but not for the first time.

I was nervously alone when I went to America. I was twenty-one. It was another turning point for me. Although it meant leaving Bess, I could not resist the opportunity to be in America at the time of the 2024 Presidential Election.

I had learned the importance of my appearance. If I was to make friends, I had to share the same sense of dress style. People like people like themselves. I put aside the wide-legged jeans and faux leather jacket that had provided a memorable image for my first year in Exeter. My birthday cash was invested in some smarter chinos and a blazer that gave me the preppy look fashionable in Washington DC and I flew to the USA for the first time.

My Uncle Brian was working in Washington and invited me

to stay for two months until Christmas, as my own parents were dealing with a crisis of their own. He was some sort of liaison officer for the Government in the mapping department, busy interpreting satellite images of Israel, Palestine and southern Ukraine, where the continuing wars and political instability were keeping the armaments industry busy and profitable.

Uncle Brian and his wife Karen were billeted in a Victorian townhouse in Georgetown, rented by the UK government for civil servants on secondment to the US. It was well furnished but had the feeling of a place to pass through, a sparse hotel, a temporary stopping-off place. It was an easy bus ride into central Washington and perfect for my stay. I needed to escape the constant kindness shown to me by Uncle Brian and Auntie Karen. They were missing the UK and the friends they had known since childhood. Karen considered me to be the only, if inadequate, substitute for her UK coffee morning friends. To escape her constant chattering about people I didn't know and was unlikely to meet, I found my place to hideaway in the bar of the Willard Hotel, close to the White House.

I loved the political buzz and found the bar at The Willard was the best place to hear the gossip and watch the candidates in huddled debates as they traded favours. On my second visit, when I explained to the barman that I was an English student of politics, he introduced me to a group of political aides who pretended an interest in the recent UK election. They welcomed me into their circle. By then, I had learned that everybody likes an audience. To be popular, I only had to listen. Hendrix, a young aide to President Biden, invited me to stay for dinner with them all. They recommended the restaurant DC Vegan, which, I was assured, was the best in Washington.

Still an occasional meat eater, but with Bess's message ringing in my ears, I readily agreed to a plant-based meal. Hendrix, they all used his middle name, was an earnest man in his late twenties. He was tall and broad-shouldered with an unruly mop of dark hair. His steel-rimmed spectacles and obligatory dark suit and white shirt suggested an academic brain and a total lack of vanity. He promised a tour of the White House the following day. Having said yes to the dinner invitation, even though they were somewhat older than me, I prepared for a boring evening. It was anything but.

The young diners were ambitious for political influence but not afraid of letting their hair down, safe in the knowledge that they were not yet significant enough for their antics to feature in newsprint. They were all full of banter and amusing gossip about the candidates and their colleagues in the White House. They all liked President Biden but were delighted that the ageing President had stood down in favour of his deputy, Vice President Kamala Harris. The prospect of a term with Republican candidate Donald Trump was too dangerous to contemplate. Hendrix said that the Democrats had done all they could to discredit Trump, but the more mud they threw, the better Trump polled.

The tension in the air was palpable as the Washington elite prepared for the job losses and promotions that followed each election. This meal had a real end-of-term feel with false laughter and unwarranted optimism. I sensed a feeling of desperation about Hendrix. He realised that his fledgling political career could soon be at an end. Time went quickly and suddenly it was too late for me to catch a bus back to Georgetown.

I hadn't enough dollars for a cab home. It was another rainy evening in Washington and I was unprepared even for the two-mile night time walk to Uncle Brian's temporary home. The group decided that I should stay in central Washington and one of them would put me up for the night. I called my Uncle Brian, who disbelieved my excuses but was more concerned and understanding than my parents would have been. Clearance to stay over was reluctantly agreed. An elaborate and often practiced knockout form of rock, paper, scissors followed with a great deal of drunken banter until eventually, by accident or design, the responsibility for my overnight stay fell to Hendrix. He said I could stay on a sofa at his apartment for the night and, with our meal finished, we rushed through the damp night streets of Washington back to his home.

When we walked into his tiny, rather shabby apartment, I sensed his unease. As Hendrix turned into his kitchenette to make two mugs of instant coffee from his hot tap, he told me that he was married with two young children at his family home in Iowa. He wanted to talk. Whether it was because of the amount of alcohol we had all enjoyed or just because of the transitory nature of our relationship, he unburdened himself to me.

Always ready to please, I was happy to listen to his rhotic accent and the alarming story he told in a gentle, wearied manner. We sat together on his tired sofa with our mugs of weak coffee as I listened. Hendrix voiced his emotions and I clearly remember the musings of a half-drunk soul feeling sorry for himself. One day, this disappointed young man would change the world with his ideas.

Hendrix had been a star pupil at Harvard and wide receiver for the very successful university football team, the Harvard Crimsons. He had dated Helen, a Harvard History of Art student and captain of Harvard Cheerleading, for eight months when she told him she was pregnant. He married her in a quiet ceremony in Cambridge, Massachusetts and flew to Iowa to meet her family. Helen's father, Nathan, was an overweight, ruddy-faced hog farmer. He was shocked and disappointed by the unexpected marriage of his daughter. Helen's mother, Janie, was just dismayed that she could not host a grand wedding breakfast. However, Helen's parents accepted Hendrix and provided a nearby cottage for them on the farm estate.

Hendrix was at first impressed by the grand family home with pilastered verandah and Dutch-style roof enclosing the vast reception areas and eight bedrooms. It was set in 2000 acres of maize, barley and wheat fields. The wealth that the farm appeared to generate and his father-in-law's reputation in St Mary's Presbyterian Church in the small nearby community of Lone Tree left Hendrix convinced that he had joined a well-respected family.

Both Helen and Hendrix were able to finish their studies at Harvard before the baby was born. Both graduated with good degrees. They returned to Iowa and soon Helen and her mother were totally engaged in decorating a nursery in the cottage and then with the new baby, William. Hendrix was commuting daily the half-hour journey into Muscatine, where he worked. He enjoyed driving the Toyota Camry borrowed from his father-in-law. He was working in a modest legal practice specialising in labour disputes. Muscatine was a small town on the Mississippi River where Hendrix barely earned his keep in the legal firm but learned a lot about people and their work-related problems.

Over dinner one Friday night, back in the family house, Nathan explained that he and other local farmers gave large political contributions both at the state and national level. They backed both Democrats and Republicans to ensure influence over whoever won the elections. That way, they had secured the Ag-Gag law in 2012 that criminalised whistleblowing in the agricultural business. This privacy law was eventually struck down as unconstitutional by the Supreme Court, but not before Nathan had increased his stock of sows by reducing the size of the farrowing crates. Doubts about the Ag-Gag law ensured that nobody would report him.

Hendrix had not yet visited the three huge barns that housed the sows. He had not even seen a pig on the farm, although Nathan boasted that he fattened 100,000 slaughter hogs a year from his 4000 gestating sows. Spurred on by the need to feel part of the family, Hendrix asked for a tour of the farm. Nathan seemed reluctant at first, but he eventually offered to show him around. The tour next day changed Hendrix's life.

The farmhouse was surrounded by corn fields. All the hogs were housed in three enormous barns in a compound encircled by barbed wire, more than a mile away from their grand home. Nathan claimed that the high level of security was to stop theft. It also discouraged activists from exposing the scenes of torture in the barns.

Outside the compound, a large sludge pool was overflowing with excrement. Its offensive smell was all-pervading as it leaked towards the Iowa River. This added a foul aroma to the already warm and humid Iowa atmosphere.

In the darkness of the barns, there were hundreds of small farrowing crates, each restraining a large breeding sow. The sows, restricted by the steel bars of the crate, could barely stand, unable to move, turn or sit with no space for their defecation. They each produced eight litters in four years.

The piglets suckled through the crate bars and then were taken from the sow after three weeks. The sows had brief relief from the crates until they were pregnant again. When they were too exhausted to continue breeding, they would be sent for slaughter. One pig caught Hendrix's attention as it gazed up at him. The sorrowful despair and sadness in the pig's blue eyes caused a welling up behind Hendrix's steel-rimmed spectacles. This fellow intelligent animal made a connection as he acknowledged their hopeless plight.

In the fattening pens, there were so many helpless animals huddled into a cramped space, pushing each neighbour as they fought their way to the feeding bins, all denied their natural habitat, not allowed to grub in a field or nurture their young. The overfed piglets were packed so tightly they could hardly move. Prematurely fattened pigs lay where they could, with legs often insufficient to carry the weight, some trampled on by fellow animals, the dead left where they fell, cannibalised by hungry neighbours. Tails had been cut off and teeth removed without anaesthetic to stop them from attacking each other. Everywhere there was the stench of faeces and the rotting corpses. The survivors were shaking in terror, scared of our presence. The pigs held their snouts aloft to avoid the excrement that remained uncleared under their feet. The walls crawled with the flies that fed from the squalor. The dirty, diseased and damaged pigs would be left in these conditions for six months until they were 120kg, large enough to be profitably slaughtered. In their own dirt and with sores and cancerous growths, the hogs looked inedible as they squabbled for space.

Then Nathan boasted how production was maximised by the sows being injected with the blood hormone PMSG, extracted from specially bred pregnant horses to stimulate and synchronise pregnancy and birth. Every day, two trucks would be loaded to transport about 300 hogs to the slaughterhouse at Edgewood, 100 miles and three crowded hours away.

Hendrix was speechless as he saw what Nathan could impose on intelligent living creatures. Here in his city apartment, Hendrix cried openly as he relived the memory of that evening, remembered the smells of death and recalled the despair he witnessed. These soulful animals were a far cry from the butchered pork and bacon slices in plastic protection that filled our supermarkets. How could this rank, putrid aroma be the smell of food? Hendrix's heart filled with despair as he realised that it was the profit from these unfortunate pigs that was funding the life he and Helen were living. Hendrix had said nothing to Nathan for fear of upsetting him yet again and was wary of his financial dependence. At that moment, he vowed to enter politics, to make a difference and bring an end to animal farming.

Hendrix and Helen had never eaten the flesh of any animal since that day, despite it being the centre piece of family meals. An unsettled tummy was his first excuse and then the claim that hogs' meat was too fatty for his delicate stomach.

After a while, Nathan and Janie accepted that Hendrix would not eat meat and that Helen supported this choice, although nothing was ever spoken.

Nathan would never admit the cruelty of his methods, would never recognise that hogs were sentient beings capable of feeling mental and physical pain. He would not be diverted from his belief that these methods were needed to feed the population. He welcomed the bucolic image of farming portrayed by the advertisers even though he knew that it was far from the truth. Being witness to the unnecessary cruelty may have contributed to his premature death.

When Joe Biden was elected President in 2020, it was Nathan's contribution to his campaign funds that secured Hendrix a job close to the Oval Office. His eyes watered with tears as he confessed that in the four years that he had been in The White House, he had made no progress in his aim to end animal farming through political intervention.

Now that his appointment was reaching an end, he probably never would. I could give him little comfort and had little understanding of the conflicting dilemmas he faced at the prospect of returning to Iowa in only a few weeks. I listened sympathetically and explained that he could only be responsible for himself. By only eating plant-based food, he at least should not feel personally guilty for the cruelty meted out by mankind to farm animals.

I bedded down on the couch, shaking away the images that

filled Hendrix's memory. I had an uncomfortable night worrying about my role in the torture and slaughter of animals. I resolved to avoid all pork, even bacon sandwiches. I wondered how marketing over the years had conspired to separate the words bacon and pork from the reality that it was pig flesh.

A whole industry ignored the cruelty and concealed the truth in the privacy of the production processing sheds. Society had accepted a misleading narrative in its selfish chase for cheap and plentiful food. I started to wonder that if we had all been so manipulated by marketing campaigns about meat products, what else was reality hidden from us? I became aware of the limitations of my education and my lack of empathy with the natural world. I was shocked and dismayed that I had allowed society to hide such secrets from me. I had become immune to the suffering Hendrix had described. What else had I failed to consider? Did I deliberately avoid unpalatable truths?

Unable to find a comfortable position on the couch, I worried about the naïveté of my world understanding. My troubled mind did not find sleep until just before I was woken by a bright and breezy Hendrix handing me another weak coffee in yesterday's mug. I did not feel ready for the exciting day ahead.

Hendrix was all smiles and charming as he showed me around the visitors' areas of the White House before the doors opened to the public. Then, with a carefree end-of-term abandon, he sneaked me into the West Wing and into the Oval Office. He quietly explained that "In here, in the calm creams and gold installed by President Biden and under the all-seeing portrait of Franklin D Roosevelt, in a room filled with photos and busts of American greats, I have totally failed to persuade our President of the need to change the American diet and methods of animal agriculture."

As Hendrix finished, I heard a soft, gentle voice saying, "We all know what to do; we just don't know how to get our party re-elected once we've done it," and I turned to see the frail frame of President Joe Biden. He had quietly entered his office. Hendrix blushed deeply and apologised. President Biden offered a benign look and asked Hendrix, "Mr. James, who is this young man privileged to sneak about in my office?" Hendrix stuttered a reply, clearly in awe of the President and nervous about what was to follow now that he had been discovered in the forbidden inner sanctuary. He explained that I was a politics student from England. The President spoke kindly of Prime Minister Starmer and we were gently ushered out of the Oval Office, for Hendrix to face his boss's admonishment and for me, regretting my crumpled shirt and unshaven face, feeling that I had touched history.

Past President Donald Trump went on to win the election after his reputation was enhanced by his reaction to two failed assignation attempts. His near-death experiences would moderate President Trump's misguided ambition and theatrical approach to his high office. It also brought an end to Hendrix James's political career, or so he thought. He would be back one day.

Chapter 6

I don't know whether to have a mid-morning coffee. Getting out of this chair is a struggle and then I'd need to visit the toilet. I'll not bother Peter. I'll just press on with my story by recalling my first attempts to find a job and to find myself.

My great, intimate adventure with Bess had ended when she and I finished University and went our different ways. She was a great girl, kind, compassionate, both earnest and frivolous. I had learned a lot from Beth, a love of nature from our long walks on nearby Dartmoor, respect for people, whatever their age, gender or ethnicity and an appreciation of animal rights, although her dancing tuition wasn't so successful. Our relationship had become, for us both, I think, mainly about sex.

Graduation day was a bit of a disappointment; more about leaving friends than celebrating the future. There was a whole world out there and we all needed to find our place in it. Bess and I had learned together and supported each other through our final university year. We were both awarded first-class honours degrees in Exeter Cathedral in front of proud parents and then we partied with each other and with Josh, who had also qualified with honours but was awarded his degree on the following day. Our families expressed their pride in our achievements with a champagne celebration before we joined more raucous friends at the Victoria Inn. Many pints of the local beer did little to improve my mood.

I said goodbye to Bess, leaving with the polite promises of keeping in touch that we both thought we would not keep. Fate would play a different hand.

A four-week cycling holiday with Josh, exploring the western coast of France and as many French girls as we could find, was soon a distant memory. I spent another long, hot summer contemplating my future, lazing at home now that University was part of my past. I didn't hear from Bess. Josh had started his placement with the Met Office in Exeter. My parents had put behind them their marital upset when Mum had been diagnosed with breast cancer, and now they only had time for themselves as they celebrated her new cure. Suddenly, my mother was the world's leading expert on the health benefits of eating lots of beans, vegetables and fruit on a plant-based diet that, together with targeted radiotherapy and immunotherapy, had saved her life. We didn't know then that genetic markers would eventually eliminate cancer in the Western world.

It was a relief to see my parents happy together, my father, with the premature balding that I would escape, and my mother now slimmer and unnaturally confident with her welcoming smile and nervous laugh. I was only interested in myself and my uncertain future.

Both my sisters were away. Amelia was taking a year off traveling in South America before University and Freya, now fifteen, was spending the whole summer with her best friend's family in their villa in the Algarve. At university, I had at first missed the hustle of home but not the constant wait for the bathroom, seeing the underwear drying on the radiators or feeling like a jealous outsider to my sisters giggled with a shared intimacy. A room of my own with polite, if sometimes chaotic, fellow students in Exeter had conditioned me for a quieter life, not the disturbance and confusion of two emotional teenage girls. Both my siblings would always be part of my life, but then I was glad they were away, giving me time to work out my future.

My family home, with its garden, spacious lawns and heated outdoor swimming pool, should have been a peaceful nirvana. It felt too quiet for me. I spent many hours in the garden, using the swimming pool when I could and helping tend the plants when it wasn't so warm. I enjoyed feeling the gentle sun on my skin and pondering my future. I listened endlessly to the cruel, haunting beauty of Beethoven's ninth symphony, relieved that I didn't share the difficulties of his life and inspired by the "Ode to Joy," which is surely the most optimistic music ever written. I learned to drive in my mother's Kia EV6, but it would be a long time before I would own a car. I missed Bess, not for her endless chatter or her future planning, but for the smell of her soap, the cuddles, her gentle hands and because music is better shared. I longed to experience a different woman. But first, I had to find work.

My opportunity came when Julia, a family friend who worked at the local vet practice, told me that they were looking for a summer receptionist. I went to meet the partners and, after a brief interview, I was offered the job on a temporary basis. When I was introduced to the vets and first met Ruth, my heart missed a beat. Newly qualified, she was only a little older than me, single, tall with dark hair and big brown eyes. Her simple pale blue clinical smock was, for me, the sexiest dress ever worn.

Ruth walked with an elegant glide and showed confidence that left me stammering in her presence. She had a passion for animals and was clearly very popular with our pet-owning clients. I couldn't sleep without thinking about her. I imagined the curves that hid beneath that smock, her nakedness in my bed and her excitement at my touch. She didn't seem to notice me. I worked on my fashion style, smiled whenever I saw her and made her morning coffee every day. Still, she didn't seem to notice. I had to do something to attract her attention. Knowing that she was on farm duty on my day off, I suggested that I shadow her to learn more about the practice. Ruth somewhat nervously agreed that I accompany her for the day.

When the time came, Ruth had dressed casually in fashionable black leggings, a simple green T-shirt and wellies. She looked like the country girl with attitude. I wore my cord trousers and a green Barbour jacket over a checked shirt as my attempt to be the country boy. Ruth cleared her desk and we set off in her old Land Rover Defender, pop music on the radio. Our first appointment was at a stud farm.

I wondered about the ethics of horse racing. Horses are the most beautiful of creatures. They clearly enjoy short gallops in the field but longer bursts of running with a jockey on board create an extra strain. They are trained for speed at the expense of bone strength.

Two hundred horses still die on the racetracks of the UK each year. I had enjoyed riding lessons at a local stable as a teenager before realising that I was too tall to be a racing jockey. I had never considered whether my horse was enjoying the experience. When we rode out, my horse, Buster, always looked pleased to turn for home and was ready to rush back more quickly than on the outward journey. I assumed that he liked his stable or the other horses in the yard, but maybe he was just happy to get me off his back.

I liked horses for their smell. For me, the smell of horses and the well-soaped leather saddle always conjured up happy memories of long gallops over open fields and quiet walks, sitting up high to see the world from a different perspective. Getting out of the car at the stables, we were struck by that earthy smell, the combination of horse manure, hay and saddle soap that characterises stables worldwide, a smell that is at the same time reassuring and unnerving.

Ruth was visiting to do an ultrasound test to see if one of the breed mares was about to ovulate. This thoroughbred mare was due to be put to Frankel, the well-known bay Derby winner of a few years earlier. I was amazed to learn that the owner of the mare would pay £125,000 per foal for its progeny.

The stud owner, a wealthy industrialist, invited us to watch a mating that was about to take place. We were shown into a viewing room by a padded stable where a frisky novice stallion was trying to mount an unwilling breed mare. When the mare was ready, the teaser stallion was taken away and the stud stallion was brought into the room. With practised experience, the stud immediately mounted the mare. Within a few moments, the mating was completed. I was left wondering how I would feel if I was prepared for intercourse by a stranger's foreplay and forced to accept a previously unseen interloper.

I was quiet as we drove to Ruth's next appointment. She looked scornfully at me as I suggested we listen to the "Barber of Seville" and turned on her pop music playlist. The upcoming consultation was at the Happy Pasture Farm. I was soon to discover the farm was neither happy nor had pasture.

The Happy Pasture Farm had a very different sound and smell to the stables. The malodorous aroma of cow excrement and petrol fumes, silage and wash-down chemicals are the unexpected industrial country smell of a twenty-first-century dairy farm.

I walked uncomfortably behind Ruth as we entered the milking parlour. Bored, emaciated cows stood in isolating stalls munching lugubriously on tired hay, moaning mournfully as they stumbled and sulked. Two of the herd of milkers had mastitis and Ruth took one look at their sunken eyes, swollen udders and walking difficulty to recognise the infection. These cows had produced watery milk with clots of puss. She prescribed a ten-day course of antibiotics. If antibiotics failed, she would remove the infected teats.

I was amazed at the size of the hanging udders, as many of the cows found it difficult to stand. A few had their hind legs shackled to stop them from doing the splits. They stood on concrete in stalls with an eating trough. They had no opportunity to interact, graze or run free. The farmer proudly explained that each cow was producing seven times its natural milk yield and that he had some milkers on their fifth lactation.

The fish meal used to complement their diet to improve yields makes the milking herds the largest oceanic predators on the planet. I was confused until he explained that each cow had to give birth annually to bring it to milk. The resultant calves were taken away so that we could drink their mother's milk. The females were sometimes retained to join the milking herd. Half of the male calves were shot at birth and half were kept isolated in cages for eight months until they were slaughtered for rose veal.

With the endless cycle of pregnancy and childbirth and udders bred to carry up to 30 litres of milk, a milking cow's life is only five years before milk yields became unprofitable. I could hear the cries of the mother cow as her useless babies were thrown into a skip. I couldn't resist gazing into the big, friendly brown eyes of one of the nameless cows and wondering what was in their minds. Acceptance is not approval.

I had become vegetarian a year earlier when Hendrix had described the horrors of his father-in-law's pig farm. Until my visit to The Happy Pasture Farm, I had no idea of the cruelty and animal pain in a dairy, another industry hiding in plain sight. I could only look myself in the mirror if I embraced a vegan lifestyle.

The dairy farmer was an abrupt conversationalist. He wore dirty boots and a well-used tweed jacket that carried his smell. He was not an attractive man. I don't think he was deliberately unkind. He was following farm practises that had been normalised by time and extended and enhanced by necessity. His grandfather had started the farm almost 80 years earlier. It had passed through the generations and, he hoped, would pass to his own son, who was currently at an agricultural college in Cirencester. Through many generations, methods have changed, but the cruelty hasn't. Factory farming had escalated cruelty.

I wondered how a whole industry could hide the truth from the public for so long. I felt a fool for not understanding that cows had to first give birth to provide milk. I felt angry that my lack of understanding was matched by almost everyone I knew. It must have been easy to hide that which we didn't want to know.

Ruth knew, as did supposedly animal-loving vets throughout the country. Her kindness and sympathetic eyes were reserved for companion animals. Behind her undoubted charm was the cruel woman who was implicit in treating friendly cows as unfeeling commodities. Vets are trained to recognise farm animals as part of the food chain, but I've never understood that a person who had devoted their studies to the welfare of animals could be so cold and unfeeling towards farm animals. At least now, I could see that my unrequited lust had been misplaced. I decided that my time at the veterinary practice had come to an end.

Chapter 7

I had been so slow to accept the cruelty of farming animals. Hendrix had told to me. Bess had lectured me. Ruth had shown me. I was still unprepared to recognise that farming animals were barbaric. I had started to follow a vegan diet, but really, all I thought about was myself and my stumbling career.

I started as a journalist in October. A lucky meeting with a neighbour in the Jolly Farmer, my local pub, provided an introduction. The Jolly Farmer was famous for its locally brewed craft ales, but I went there for the company. The county had lost much of the farmland as it had developed grand country houses in large plots and pretty towns with good access to London business communities. Many hectares of Surrey woodland and moorland were used for military training for the soldiers at Aldershot. There were not many farmers left in Surrey and the Jolly Farmer catered for business leaders and young hopefuls, like me.

One of my drinking partners, Philip, a recruitment agent, knew of an opportunity and after his introduction, I became a freelance journalist working exclusively for the online magazine Metascope. Philip must have recognised my practised skill as a listener. I did find everybody interesting once I had discovered what interested them. In the end, there wasn't much listening to do to fulfil my role at Metascope.

My job was to report on the social life of celebrities. I set up a desk in a bedroom in my parents' house. After an early morning run, a welcomed shower and my predictable breakfast of tomatoes on toast, I was always at my desk by 9:00 am, Classic FM on the radio. I wrote stories by trawling through the digital media provided by celebrities about themselves. I calculated that by using ChatGPT, I could collect background facts and have my articles written and edited by AI.

Published articles would add to the Chatbot knowledge and when checked, probably on ChatGPT, my contribution would be part of the accumulated knowledge and, therefore, the new reality. I need not be restricted by facts.

As I described the evermore promiscuous activities of the beautiful people in the spotlight, I still felt frustrated by my own lack of adventure, lack of a cause and lack of direction. Was I always someone looking on from the sidelines, never part of the real action, the audience, not the performer? But this was to change after I read an article written by the Speciesism activist Susan Clarke and published in the Guardian's online newscast. I have kept a copy: -

It was about seven years ago that I realized the pain and suffering that I had been causing by my diet. Whilst I had been campaigning against fox hunting and vivisection, my knife and fork had been responsible for so many more atrocities against animals. I fell into deep despair, despair about what I had done, despair about the ignorance that had allowed it, despair about the animal farming that created it, the advertising industry that hides it and a government that ignores it.

The more I investigated, the more horrified I became as I realised the huge Holocaust of animal agriculture is also the biggest threat to our very existence because of the way it pollutes, causes global warming, squanders scare resources of land and water and the way it destroys the habit of all species until all too soon it will destroy our own.

I could not understand how my friends wouldn't see what had become so obvious to me. I shouted at my meat-eating family. My friends' behaviour appalled me. I was in a dark and lonely place, consumed by disappointment in myself and the whole human race. I had lost all confidence.

And then, I found a group of people who could imagine the possibilities of a universal plant-based diet. Food supplies enough to feed the world's growing population, the restoration of habitat that will enable all species to live in harmony and re-wilding that will absorb Carbon emissions to halt global warming need only a change of diet. These people are making a difference. The world is at last opening up to its message. Nobody can deny the evidence. People can no longer say, "I didn't know."

We can create the Modern Utopia that, in 1905, HG Wells predicted would follow the closing of the last slaughterhouse.

The article inspired me to think that I could emulate Bob Woodward or Carl Bernstein and expose the great industrial conspiracies that determined our lifestyles. This article echoed my experiences. With Susan Clarke's words ringing in my ears, I fantasised that I would expose the serpentine relationships between big business and governments that erased the truth about animal farming and skewed the subsidy system to favour farm animal cruelty. I would change the world with my journalism. And then the candles struck again.

Metascope was sued for deformation and I was named as the errant journalist. A minor celebrity claimed that my published article about her relationship with an adult porn star was damaging her career and that I had made it up. The two had been photographed together arm in arm and I admit guessing the rest. I was fired and Metascope defended the action, leaving me worried about my behaviour once again. My birthday candle luck was following me around, but soon it was to change because then I met Mia.

Chapter 8

Since Bess, I had not really connected with anybody. All the women I fancied turned out to be gay. I didn't connect with men and couldn't find a love of football that seemed to be the language of my gender. I didn't think that I was gay, but I started to wonder. Why do we have so many insecurities and uncertainties when we are young?

I wasn't surprised when Mia, a well-known influencer, approached me to advance her image in "Metascope." Minor celebrities contacted me all the time, but I was impressed when her messages moved to speaking by phone and eventually to a date.

We first met at Gordon Ramsay's latest Vegan restaurant in Tottenham, London's newest hotspot. Mia was beautiful, with little make-up and the whitest teeth I have ever seen. She was quite small but had perfect proportions that suited her simple dress style. Her long dark hair and olive skin gave her the chaste appearance of a Victorian country girl with the serenity imagined by Sir John Everett Mills in his painting of Ophelia. Her outdoor appearance masked a sophisticated manner and a taste for high-end eating that was unusual for a young girl and certainly new to me. I pretended a knowledge of food as we ordered the menu of the day and I remained unsure of what I had eaten, even after the meal had finished.

Over an exceptional spread of stuffed morel with white asparagus followed by potato gnocchi with Spring vegetables and wild garlic, Nova asked me about my life story and gently explained her own. The daughter of an alcoholic actress and a moderately successful illustrator of children's books, Mia was creative with a childlike simplicity. Her real passion was clothing design, but she was about to host a television reality programme about new architecture.

It seems strange now, but in 2026, houses were still being built outside in the open air in all weathers. Then, it was almost always cold or wet. Mia was championing fully equipped kit houses built in a factory.

We got on really well as we shared stories of our experiences and found we had much in common, but I could tell that there was no romantic interest. Over dinner, Mia suggested I should become a fashion model as I had an interesting face and a perfect tall, slender body. She promised me some introductions, but I took no notice. I promised her some media cover if I could, and we agreed to meet again, dinner this time my treat.

Our second meeting was almost a month later. Metascope had published a flattering interview with Mia that I had fabricated before I had been dismissed. She came with her partner. Nova was older, maybe thirty, as tall as me with a thin, angular body, high cheekbones and short-cropped blond hair. She was striking in a pink trouser suit with a grey scarf. Her matching grey shoes had the highest heels I had ever seen. She walked with a confidence that I wrongly associated with haughtiness.

I soon learned that Nova was the owner of the modelling agency “Masquerade.” Nova took one look at me, turned to Mia, gave her a big kiss and said, “You’ve found him for me.” Nova offered me a job. I couldn’t let them down. Unemployed and with the threat of legal action hanging over me, I felt that the candles had at last been thwarted by this unexpected opportunity. The promised money was mouth-watering, and I signed up for her agency the following day. My lofty ambitions to change the world had been quickly overtaken by the prospect of money and glamour. From then onwards Mia, Nova and I were always friends.

Having a ready income and financial prospects, I rented my first independent home, a studio apartment in a converted warehouse building in Carlow House Camden, Northwest London. The rent for this tiny Manhattan-style apartment stretched my income, but I had confident expectations and no responsibilities. I decorated the brick walls with posters of the artworks of the impressionists Monet and Renoir and filled the space with the sounds of Mozart in a move that signalled my pretentious early life.

Being in the fashion industry encouraged my love of high-end clothes. Some were given after a shoot, but most I had to buy from my generous fees. Suits from William Westmacott in Saville Row, handmade shoes from Tom

Ford and shirts from Hermes soon filled my bedsit wardrobe. I thought that I was living my best life.

I often met Nova and Mia for a catch-up over coffee or, sometimes, dinner, but I especially remember our celebration dinner when Mia was appointed Communications Director of Jaguar Land Rover. The company had been a car manufacturer until the CEO, Arshia Kapoor, recognised that the worldwide demand for cars was diminishing as electric vehicles could not provide the same flexibility or status symbol as the predecessor petrol cars. High costs, the growth in public transport and shared car ownership schemes were throttling the traditional car manufacturing industry. Ms. Kapoor had realised that there was a substantial shortage of homes and was changing all Jaguar Land Rover production facilities in the UK to the production of modular houses and flats.

Arshia Kapoor could not have found a better spokesperson than the charismatic Mia, who was soon to become a household name. I often wondered if her diminutive appearance helped her presentation because her petite frame made the rooms in the houses look enormous as she walked around them.

Over our dinner at Mallow in London's Borough Market, Mia explained that the real game changer had been the creation of a paint that contained photovoltaic cells that captured the light and converted it into electricity. The Jaguar housing modules were self-sufficient in energy. Jaguar was producing 500,000 fully equipped modules a year that would form around 100,000 dwellings, depending on how they were connected. Production line facilities and repetition made them cheap to build, whilst the design ensured connectivity however the modules were assembled, allowing variation in the final home. They had partnered with the major developers who would provide the land and infrastructure. It was Nova who made them popular with her promotions and I think that she and Jaguar can be credited with solving the housing crisis that had made house ownership so difficult through the decade.

Mia was away when Nova asked me to partner with her at dinner with a number of wealthy potential investors in her modelling agency. I was seated next to Ranjit Singh, the owner of Smiley Egg, a major egg and poultry producer. Now, it's hard to believe that chicken and eggs were part of our staple diet or to understand how we ignored the brutish primitive conditions of animal farming approved by government regulators. Over dinner, I listened with practised intensity as Ranjit explained that after three consecutive years of bird flu, he was having to destroy his flocks. Together with high fuel costs and declining demand, the bird flu was destroying his business and his wealth. He had decided to convert all his bird sheds to the production of mushrooms.

The health benefits of speciality mushrooms such as Turkey Tail and Lions Mane had been widely accepted and prices were rising. Mushrooms would thrive in the dark, damp spaces that had been home to the one billion chickens slaughtered in the UK each year.

Although I took a dislike to the self-confident Midlander, I didn't think him a brutal man. He confessed that he had never been in any of his immense chicken barns. If he had he would have seen the conditions that he had presided over. He would have smelt the odour of rotting flesh and the high stink of chicken excrement, left where it lay. He would have faced the sound of millions of chickens crowded together, squawking for space. He would have seen young chicks overfed for four weeks so that their legs could not hold their body weight, dying in the crush, bullied by birds rubbing too close together to form feathers. If he had visited his egg-producing facilities he would have seen how all the male chicks were transported down conveyor belts to be macerated alive in giant mixers, their crushed bodies bagged and sent to zoos and pet food shops. He would have seen how five hens are crowded into a cage about 35cm square with cages piled on top of each other in rows longer than a football pitch. He would be told the ruthless way that his facilities, like all egg production sheds, expected that each hen would produce a totally unnatural three hundred eggs each year. He would have understood how such proliferation of production brought premature death for his stock of egg layers who would only survive for twelve months.

It was profit, not compassion, that was delivering change, but I was excited that fewer living creatures would be victims of our demand for cheap food.

Chapter 9

I think that I will have that coffee-flavoured energy drink now. Peter will bring it for me. He will have finished upstairs. After all, he only needed to make my bed and switch the ventilation system to "clean". I will play some music. I like to concentrate on the sounds, to let the instruments wash over me. I don't usually like background music as I think it is disrespectful to the composer and performers, but today, I must make an exception. With limited time I must try to multi-task.

I can't help but look back to a time when I was younger. I wish now that I had relaxed and had more fun during my time modelling. I thought that I was happy at the time, but looking back, I wonder why I had taken myself so seriously. I was well paid with even better expenses. I enjoyed international travel to often glamorous locations and stayed in good hotels. Lots of very pretty girls wanting a distraction from the boredom of the daily photoshoot could have been more available. Embarrassing casting auditions and unexplained rejections served to provide contrast to the compliment of being "just right" for the intended promotion. I was still only 25 and I should have been having a ball, but I was a serious young man, caught up in politics since my university days. I was fascinated by the recognition that major change needed political intervention and I felt desperate for the intelligent leadership that was missing. So many solutions always felt obvious to me and I couldn't comprehend the lack of understanding by our politicians. Why can't they see the wood for the trees and provide simple solutions that we could all understand? The confidence of youth remains with me in old age.

I was away on a photo shoot in Barbados with six beautiful girls for the annual Pirelli calendar when the UK election was called. Wild seas on the east coast of Barbados had made swimming impossible. However, it provided a great backdrop for some raunchy art pictures. I was very much a bit player in the shoot because most of the pictures showed sexy poses with girls that would end up in workshops and building sites around the world. Pirelli did not wish to appear misogynistic as they published their calendar. Therefore included some shots with me to provide the balance. We stayed at the expensive Sandy Lane Hotel on the west coast. Pirelli was covering our expenses.

The hotel was already planning sea-breakers to conserve the beautiful white sandy beach in the light of increasing sea levels. Changing patterns of sea currents and increased humidity in the warmer air had already made the Caribbean islands more vulnerable to extreme weather events. Our visit was before the traditional hurricane season, but the increasing incidence of hurricanes in the Caribbean was already affecting the holiday trade. Even the Sandy Lane Hotel decor was beginning to look tired and the garden palm trees had been stripped of their fronds by untamed winds.

Gritty sands were swirling over uncertain beaches where unsettled waves, even in sheltered bays, made a lie of holiday brochure photographs. Rising temperatures, increasing sea levels, tropical storm surges, coastal erosion, droughts and flooding were all forecast for the future. The Barbadian tree-planting policy would do little to avoid the worst impact on the local economy. On a calm day, I was glad to swim in the sea before the degraded marine system would desecrate the planet's most valuable asset.

I was bored by yet another photo shoot with a gay director, competitive backbiting girls and a geeky camera crew. My political enthusiasm, fostered in Exeter, ensured that I took a close interest in the UK election. With his popularity plunging after failing to deliver on his manifesto promises, Kier Starmer had resigned in favour of Jonathon Reynolds shortly before the election campaign started. Kier Starmer was another politician to over-promise and underachieve. Jonathon Reynolds was a centrist with some radical ideas to meet the challenge of Nigel Farage's Reform UK Party.

A resurgent Conservative party also faced fierce competition for right-of-center votes from Reform. None of the parties campaigned for environmental change. All re-affirmed their commitment to zero CO_2 emissions by 2050 but didn't detail a scheme to reach carbon neutrality other than a proliferation of wind farms to provide energy security.

Some success was claimed, but it was our decline in manufacturing that exported our emissions by replacing UK production elsewhere. There seemed to be no government recognition of the contribution of animal farming to the ever-increasing greenhouse gasses, overuse of water, land erosion and pollution.

Jonathon Reynolds had chosen the middle ground in politics. His strength in economic affairs, his confident delivery of the speeches, and name recognition had earned him some credit with an electorate wanting stability. With the centre-right vote split, voting by sixteen-year-old voters for the first time, the continued growth of the Green Party and a reduced Liberal Democrat turnout, the electorate gave an unpopular Labour Party a second term in office.

Jonathon Reynolds entered 10 Downing Street with uncertain support but renewed hope for a fairer and kinder country. He had a mandate for the radical policies to simplify taxation and benefits that he had planned as Secretary of State for Business and Trade.

In his first 100 days, Jonathon Reynolds' new Chancellor, Greg Hands, doubled the Personal Allowance to £25000 to remove another two million people from the tax system, raised the basic tax rate to 25% and the threshold for the new 50% higher rates of taxation to £75000. Capital gains tax would be treated as income and taxed accordingly. These measures were broadly seen as tax-neutral and accepted by the city and the population as a move in the right direction to simplify taxation and reduce the size of government administration in view of continuing labour shortages.

To encourage the growth of the electric car ownership she scraped the annual Vehicle Tax and replaced it with a £2 per litre addition to exercise duty on petrol and diesel oil. This measure would recover a similar tax revenue as the Vehicle Tax until the consumption of fossil fuels was replaced by electricity. A register of car ownership was to be held by the police.

The move to encourage electric car ownership was applauded by environmentalists, as was his long-established policy to increase land, wind and solar energy development. Less popular amongst his supporters was the decision not to pursue the abolition of the House of Lords or the devolution of further powers from Westminster.

Chapter 10

I take my coffee drink in my favourite old pottery mug. I bet the mug is worth something now. Since plastics were banned and cups were largely made from cellulose structures, the drinks never cooled quickly enough for me. Some things were better in the past, particularly my mug. I have time to spend a few moments listening to the bright instrumental effects of Vivaldi's musical interpretation of Spring and it instantly reminds me of the new life I will not see. Today, even happiness makes me sad.

General economic activity did seem to be improving in the country when Jonathon Reynolds was appointed Prime Minister. I remember sharing in the swelling optimism that the country enjoyed. We were at last feeling prosperous. Consumerism created jobs and the high fashion that paid my wages. World poverty was far from a thing of the past, but in Western economies, we enjoyed all the happiness money could bring. Then, I faced the stark reality of the climate change crisis.

It was 2028 when I got caught up in the fear of climate change. I attended COP34 in Sydney, Australia, for a photo shoot. We stayed at the Park Hyatt Hotel, overlooking Sydney harbour. Amongst all the guests the talk was of the revision of the global warming targets. For each of the three previous years, the world had surpassed the long-held plan to restrict warming to 1.5 degrees above pre-industrial levels. The 2027 statistics recorded the hottest year on record, with global temperatures recorded as 1.75 degrees above the pre-industrial 19th-century average. Sea levels had risen by 17 cm since the turn of the century. The world population had grown to 8.5 billion.

Australia, with the growth of its large areas of arid land, was facing the severe consequences of global warming. The COP 34 host country had suffered a big reduction in the tourist trade now that the coral reef had disappeared, and Kakadu National Park no longer had animals. Sydney was suffering intense heat waves and the constant threat of bushfires. Coastal holiday homes were threatened by flooding from rising sea levels. The heatwaves had severely reduced the land available for agriculture. The weather conditions in central Australia were too hot for the growth of any form of pasture and, of course, for animal habitation.

Reductions in fossil fuel consumption had slowed the mining industry to almost a standstill but had not been enough to slow the temperature rise. The promised space electricity stations would come on stream by 2035, but there was still uncertainty as to the environmental impact of transmission through the atmosphere. The giant reflectors being built in India and marine cloud brightening had not yet made any significant slowing to the temperature of Earth. Some large-scale carbon capture installations had been approved in the US and UK, but financing was proving difficult in spite of government subsidies. Nobody had a solution.

My photo shoot was to promote clothes by Lawrence made from bamboo. The death of Putin and the end of the war in Ukraine had brought a return to European prosperity. With a rising Stock Exchange and a warmer climate came shorter dresses and more freedoms. The models with me for the shoot wore dresses in line with the then-current fashion that less is more. Their dresses revealed almost all of their body through sheer, transparent and clingy material. They all had the slim figure, firm breasts and the confidence to feel good almost naked. I noticed the admiring glances from many of the 40,000 delegates who had assembled in Australia to make excuses about the lack of progress in reducing greenhouse gasses. Despite all the bad news, the many delegates enjoying their expenses paid a visit to Sydney made for a heady occasion. Because I was accompanying the girls, I was a popular guest at the parties. I attended a party every night for our two-week' shoot. Whilst the girls flirted with the many men who wanted to share their beds, I was an anonymous partygoer. And then I met Jessica.

Jessica was an Israeli entrepreneur. She owned a company that was producing dairy free milk from microbes by precise fermentation. The company was supplying the major chocolate manufacturers who could use this milk without changing their recipes or taste and enjoy substantial cost savings. With memories of Ruth and the cruelty of dairy farming still ringing in my brain, I was intrigued by Jessica. It helped that she had beautiful brown eyes, a clear complexion, perfect manners and that she talked to me as though I was the only person in the room. Her eyes sparkled with emotion as she discussed her business and how it would change the world. Cheap substitute dairy products would allow cows a natural life away from the exploitation of the dairy industry. She could not understand how the environmental delegates were still largely ignoring the contribution made by unsustainable animal farming to the damaging greenhouse gasses and unsustainable environmental damage. Jessica was attending COP34 to plead the environmental case for plant-based food strategies.

Later that night, I went invited, to her room overlooking Sydney Harbour at the Four Seasons Hotel. Jessica wore an elegant cream gown that was a pleated band of sheer mesh fabric held at the back by a narrow shoulder strap. The dress revealed her slender figure and much of her long legs. I was immediately aroused as she looked so beautiful and so sexy, her olive skin highlighted by the transparent cream material of her dress. She looked at me and let the dress slide to the floor to lay bare her sun-tanned body, leaving me embarrassed by the extent and obviousness of my desire. When we were in bed together, she was kind and gentle. Her considerate lovemaking reminded me of Bess. I realised what I had missed during the last two years. I had wondered about my own sexual preferences. I had been surrounded by the young attractive models but failed to see them as sexual partners. I knew that it was love that I wanted.

Chapter 11

My time with those beautiful models was probably better than I now remember. How I wish that I could feel as lively as I did then. Although I understood the environmental cost of travel, I continued to persuade myself that there was nothing I could do personally to create meaningful change. My modelling career took me all over Europe and sometimes further afield. I remember little but anonymous hotels, the boredom of waiting for another shoot, listening to the bitchy complaints of art directors, cameramen and makeup artists and partying with ambitious and fun-loving models. I do, however, remember Berlin in the summer of 2030.

It was autumn when I took my early morning run around the streets of Berlin, alone but unconcerned for my safety in this friendly city. I marvelled at the diverse architecture. Prussian palaces sit alongside uncompromising modern buildings, many displaying the brutalism of the Nazi years. Leaves, fallen from the ever-present linden trees, brushed along the wide pavements, leaving large piles waiting to be collected in the daily clean up. Sparrows, Nuthatch and Great Tits cling to the roadside trees, their calls competing with the quiet traffic to attract attention. The sun made its early start to sparkle the streets, still wet from yesterday's showers and, as my pace slackened, I felt remarkably lucky to be in this wonderful, vibrant city at a time of plenty.

The whole team was booked into the Adlon Kempinski

Hotel, a big brutal building where the service provided the well-renowned German efficiency, with an unusual politeness usually only found in Spanish hotels. Because of the beautiful women in our group, we were admitted to the Berghain, Berlin's most famous night spot. The pounding music and startling techno consumed my very body and I had never experienced such a high. Mozart would have approved of Lady Machine. I danced all night and early into the morning. I left at sunrise, sucking in the mild temperature, delighted to find a dry day and feeling especially content.

I was abruptly brought to my senses when I looked in a small art gallery where the original AI art of Stephanie Lane was on display. Her images of women and babies thrust into the lifestyles of farmed animals were beautiful and alarming in equal measure. I bought an original Stephanie Lane when I could hardly afford it and had nowhere to hang it. I never regretted my purchase. The disturbing image is of a young girl, newly pregnant, connected to a milking machine. The haunted expression on her accepting face captured the dismal plight of the dairy cow I had met on my day with Ruth. I wanted to cry. Stephanie Lane's work demonstrated the brutality of animal agriculture and the need to bring an end to the speciesism that allows it.

How could this exquisite world allow itself to be threatened by all this unacknowledged cruelty and unkindness? Cruelty in plain sight was the mark of humanity in the early part of this century.

Chapter 12

I am sitting here now, as I have done for so many years, at the desk I bought in Farnham and in the comfort of the old leather captain's chair I had bought before I learned of the evils of the leather trade. The light from the window sparkles on the frame of a photograph of my constant companion golden retriever, Saffron. The picture sits on a table beneath a David Hockney poster of Nichols Canyon 1980.

Together, they remind me of the affection possible between humans and other animals and the complexity of the beauty that surrounds us. Even now, we still measure progress in terms of technology, physical achievement and wealth generation. I think that this century's greatest achievement is the sense of the beauty of the natural surroundings that we are protecting and the kindness and inclusion that has so much reduced animal slaughter. I am ruminating on what I will miss, but back to my story. I must mention the Coronation of our late King.

I had always admired the Royal Family as a tourist attraction, and particularly King Charles, who had such a disappointing life, struck by illness so soon after his long-awaited opportunity had arisen. With time on my hands, I wanted to be in London for the coronation of King William V, interrupting my international travel and supposed jet-set lifestyle. My visit gave me the chance to catch up with my old friend Josh.

I had kept in regular contact with Josh. He had married for the second time after a gentle divorce from his early childless marriage, but he spoke little of his new wife, Ava, whom I had not yet met. He kept me informed of his career changes as he progressed in the space travel industry. Josh had come to believe that this planet was doomed by human overconsumption and that the survival of the species was dependent on finding resources on other planets. In this way, he reconciled his environmental concerns with the consumption of resources demanded by space travel. Maybe he will be proven right one day.

Interest in commercial space tourism was waning as early experiments had failed. Innovative change and progress had slowed. The total dependence of the Western world on satellite technology had increased the risk of space warfare. When Josh turned up at Waterloo Station, his crumpled appearance was unchanged from his childhood days. There was the inevitable apple bulging in his suit pocket. His busy brain was disguised by his vacant stare. I loved that man for his simple constancy and immense intelligence. He explained that his company had directed its attention to defence equipment. Orbital weapons systems capable of retaliation in the event of a satellite attack were in design stages in the UK. The cost of travel through gravity made ground-based missiles much less effective than satellite-based weapons. Although the 1967 Outer Space Treaty, signed by over one hundred countries, prohibited the building of weapons of mass destruction in space, the government felt the necessity to be prepared in case a rogue state ignored the space law.

Josh's release from his daily worries took the form of an intense passion for football and Exeter City Women in particular. I imagine it was encouraged by Ava as he had shown no inclination for sport when we were at university. Anyway, he had certainly found a new interest and Exeter City were top of the league now that they were owned by the AI entrepreneur Elijah Carson. Josh was also keen to discuss the apple green 2025 Porsche E911 that he was restoring. Josh was enjoying a much fuller life than me.

Josh was playing an important part in the protection of our future whilst I was just standing around having my photograph taken. I wondered what he thought of me. He never criticised. I sensed that he thought that I had allowed myself to be seduced by money and fame. I had planned to expose the advertising industry that now provided my income and lifestyle. Whatever disappointment he felt in me, he still joined me for a reunion in London to celebrate the Coronation.

King Charles III had already made a substantial reduction in the Royal Civil List and the Sovereign Grant, often at the cost of family relationships. William was going to reduce the number of Royal households and carry out all his duties from Buckingham Palace.

The Coronation was a modest ceremony. The shortened procession had all the precision the reduced military forces could muster. King William wore a simple but immaculately tailored morning suit and white shirt, a break from the tradition of a military uniform. William would not be a theatrical Head of State. Tall and slender Queen Katherine cast an elegant figure at his side.

The late King's widow, Queen Camila, now to revert to her title Duchess of Cornwall, was present but did not appear on the ceremonial balcony. She returned to the quiet life she had enjoyed before being thrust into the unwanted limelight. Prince Harry, Duke of Sussex, bald and going to fat, was a tired and lonely figure as he watched his brother swear the Coronation Oath that had been used since 1688.

After his divorce from Megan, Duchess of Sussex, Prince Harry had returned to the UK to live a secluded life with his children. The Press had respected his right to privacy when his mental health diagnosis had been revealed. Harry's childhood trauma, his military service, his estrangement from family and his acrimonious divorce had all played a part in damaging a young man who had once shown so much energy.

Though reduced in size, the coronation had all the pomp and ceremony that was prized in the UK. Gold carriages, pulled by thoroughbred horses. Young men, bullied to look like toy soldiers, paraded before cheering crowds, keeping in step behind sweating portly officers whose straining uniforms were trying to escape their restricting belts.

The diamond-encrusted crown placed on the bald head of the new king only served to ridicule the process that celebrated the political impotence of the UK head of state. King William respected the traditional ceremony but introduced a clearer understanding of the role in modern society. He caught the mood of the nation when he announced that only the Monarch, his wife Queen Katherine, and George, the new Prince of Wales, would carry out Royal duties and be in receipt of Sovereign Grants. There would be no appointment of Ladies in Waiting, and the Royal household staffing would be greatly reduced. His mother, the ill-fated Princess Diana, would have been proud to see him.

After seeing the procession from Westminster Abbey to Buckingham Palace and cheering the balcony party, Josh and I took ourselves to the Horse and Guardsman, a Victorian pub in Whitehall near Horse Guards Parade. Over a few pints of the traditional brew and a plate of spiced cauliflower, spinach and lentil pie, followed by baked apple with vegan custard, we reminisced about our college days and speculated about the future. Josh was convinced that we would soon make contact with another planet. Artificial Intelligence had enabled the recognition of more matter in our own planetary system and new black holes were being revealed as scientists searched for answers. Jupiter's moon, Europa, had revealed a salty Earth-like seawater below the frozen surface that could sustain life forms. Surely, we were not the only inhabitants of the Universe. The search for interplanetary connection had been progressing since the beginning of the twentieth century. Josh was obsessed with the search for alien life. It was to be another thirty years before signals would be heard. Josh would be amongst the first to interpret the messages from Kepler-452b that would send shock waves through the world we knew.

Chapter 13

The day seems to rush by when your time is running out. I may not be able to finish my story if I take too many breaks, but it must be time for my lunchtime glass of red wine. Few believe me, but my claim that good health depends on a shot glass of British olive oil in the morning and two glasses of good English Merlot at lunchtime seems to have worked. I am reluctant to play more music. Mozart's Eine Kleine Nachtmusik will have my eyelids drooping in five minutes. Maybe midday is a little too early for lunch, so let me tell you about my next real love.

I will never get Caitlin out of my head, even though, in so many ways, she was such a disappointment. It is hard to explain my infatuation because she was selfish and cruel towards me but she remained like a sparkling jewel, the sun to my moon. I was in love with the public Caitlin, tall, elegant, sophisticated, immaculately dressed, cultured, knowledgable and constantly polite. Her short bob hairstyle and perfect makeup emphasised her high cheekbones, narrow nose and full lips. Caitlin was classically beautiful. It was later that I realised that her smile never reached her eyes. She never liked music, but I didn't recognise the emotional repression it could have signalled. The hotel hid the murmur of service behind a constant background of unemotional lift music, chosen by Caitlin, but she never lost herself in the passion of opera, the romance of an orchestra, or even the accessible sounds of Justin Bieber or Maren Morris.

Her easy manner and engaging personality were, reserved for her customers and the public spaces. Our early encounters were a pretence. Caitlin was a different person in the privacy of our hotel suite.

I met Caitlin at a photo shoot in Norfolk, where I was modelling the lightweight waterproof country wear that had become so popular for everyday use, even in the cities. All the photo shoot team were all staying at the new spa hotel at Sandringham, the Royal Estate that King William had sold shortly after his coronation. Caitlin was the manager of the hotel. At 36, she was a little older than me, but, like me, she had not been married.

The Sandringham Hotel had been bought as a flagship property by Jin Jiang International, the world's biggest hotel chain, based in Shanghai. The hotel group had spent one hundred million pounds on buying the red brick Sandringham House with its fifty-acre garden. The six hundred acre parkland and the rest of the twenty thousand acres of the Sandringham Estate had been converted to a re-wilding project favoured by the new Monarch.

The hotel chain had spent a further large fortune on refurbishing the 19th-century house into a contemporary hotel and converting the many grand rooms into three opulent restaurants. The Michelin three-star Vegan Royal Restaurant, the obligatory traditional Chinese restaurant and the European Bistro were a highlight of the hotel. King William had given his approval to the Royal name as he and Queen Katherine had both been vegan for many years after Katherine's own cancer diagnosis. The King had banned hunting, shooting and fishing on the royal estates, even though these had been the chosen pursuits of his predecessors. Caitlin's job was to fill the thirty-bedroom suites and make a return on the investment.

Already rising sea levels were threatening large areas of Norfolk, reducing tourism once the curiosity of visiting a royal house was sated. The house itself would be underwater by 2065 as warmer seas, storm surges and the ice cap melt continued.

My refusal to model for any items including animal products, had earned me a reputation of being awkward and difficult to manage. I had learnt that the chemicals and treatment for preparing and tanning leather were one of the most polluting industries on the planet. Much of the treatment was done in Indian sweatshops, feeding untreated waste into the great river Ganges, even though it was already one of the most polluted rivers in the world. As a result of the process, there was very high levels of illness and premature death among the badly paid leather industry workforce.

The fox and racoon dog fur farms of Finland, Canada and China, were producing about five million fox and racoon pelts each year. The dogs were bred and kept in small cages and then killed by anal electrocution. It made me face up to the cruelty of breeding animals just for furs to adorn beautiful people. I felt that I had no alternative but to stand against the unnecessary use of animal products in the fashion industry. The fashion trend was towards cruelty-free fashion fake furs, although leather still played a big part in men 's clothing and shoes. My ethical beliefs were reducing my income without receiving any recognition. There was not enough work to keep me fully occupied. With my modelling career starting to stumble now that most fashion houses were designing for the fuller figure, I needed to find an alternative way of life.

Something clicked inside me as soon as I saw into Caitlin 's intelligent blue eyes and heard the soft Irish lilt in her voice. It might have been love. I couldn't believe that she wasn't already married or that she had time for me. Soon, we were inseparable, checking into competitor's restaurants for dinner, sharing breakfast in the hotel, meeting for early evening cocktails and taking private walks in the gardens and grounds. We discussed politics, economics, and business. We gossiped about the places we had visited and the people we knew. I could sense that Caitlin was ready for a lasting relationship. At last, I had found my voice and somebody to listen to me. My happiness would only last a few weeks.

Caitlin was respected and liked by her staff. I was in love with her elegance and her conversation, as well as her grace and refined taste. My desire was fuelled by her inaccessibility until, one evening, she invited me to her private suite at the Sandringham. I was overwhelmed by the sophistication of her decor and the opulence of these surroundings. I imagined living with this graceful, stylish partner and although I knew very little about her, I felt as though she would always look after me, as indeed, she did. I proposed after four weeks. I never thought to enquire whether she also wanted children.

We married secretly in the local Register Office by special licence. I moved out of my rental apartment in Camden and into the Manager's suite at the hotel. The staff insisted on providing us with a wedding party, but I sensed that it was given with some uncertainty and suspicion. Caitlin put me on the payroll as a Welcomer and Host, tasked with greeting guests, a role at which I excelled once I had a full knowledge of the hotel, its history, its gardens, food and wine cellar. My chameleon character was ideally suited to the role. We would have thirteen eventful years of married life together, during which I had fewer dalliances than she did.

I quickly adapted to her routine. Caitlin would breakfast early on fruit and peppermint tea. She would meet with each of her managers daily for fifteen minutes before they started their shifts. In my formal slot, I was informed of all incoming guests, their history, likes and preferences. Caitlin's lunch was always a green salad with a lemon dressing and a jug of iced water with cucumber, taken alone in one of the dining rooms. Each evening, I would join her for one of the restaurant meals to sample the fare before service started. She seldom finished the plate and maintained her slim figure.

Behind Caitlin's graceful elegance, she had an urgent need to throw off her inhibitions in violent sex play. At first, our lovemaking was kind and gentle. After only two weeks I could see Caitlin was bored by my conventional approach. She showed me some of the positions she had learned on her international travels. Some I enjoyed, but soon she wanted to dress up for me. Little girl outfits, crotchless police uniforms and fishnet body stockings started to appear. I thought it humiliating that sharing natural lovemaking was insufficient for her. Although I felt uncomfortable, I went along with the roleplaying as my life at the hotel was so easy. My daytime was spent in the gym and swimming pool, reading in the hotel library or walking in the estate. Every evening, we would dress to play elegant hosts to our guests in the hotel.

Caitlin was a jealous woman and felt threatened anytime she found me talking to a young female customer. She accused me of swimming to show off my body and soon insisted that I only used the pool when it was closed to guests. Daytime and evenings, we remained the elegant, loving couple, dressed formally to entertain our customers at the hotel. In the bedroom, Caitlin wanted a less sophisticated adventure. Now, I can't imagine why I didn't stop being her fetish fantasy earlier, but at the time, my confidence was falling and I couldn't see other options. One afternoon, before our hotel round, when Caitlin asked me to wear her lingerie under my tuxedo and I vowed to stop the madness.

I knew what an asset I was for Caitlin and the hotel as I mingled with the customers that evening, listening attentively to their stories. When we returned to our suite, I told Caitlin that I could no longer be her sex toy. My vanity hated the idea of failure but could not accept being dominated by Caitlin. She was very understanding and quick to accept my rejection. She arranged a second room for me and said that so long as I didn't expose the truth or embarrass her, we could continue our pretended perfect marriage. She was planning to return to her previous arrangement with the head chef, Aurora, who had regularly shared her room before our marriage. Caitlin knew that her Chinese masters would not approve of her same-sex relationship with Aurora and I was to be her perfect cover. I was too ashamed and too proud to admit these arrangements to anybody, not even Josh, who could only assume that I had a happy marriage.

I still loved the public Caitlin for her self-assurance and personal discipline. It flattered my ego to be seen alongside this elegant and successful woman, even though we were displaying a false impression. Or was it? In public I was sharing my life with the public woman I loved. It was an arrangement that could work.

Our marriage would continue for years but it had really ended in just six weeks. My dream of a son with Caitlin was lost. Had I made another mistake or just been caught up by the curse of the candles? Once again, nothing was quite what it appeared to be.

My promise of faithfulness lasted about three days. I was swimming naked at night in the pool closed to guests. I was vigorously splashing my crawl up and down the quiet water, feeling its ozone freshness, when Aurora walked in wearing only a tiny black thong. She had started her night time swimming routine rather earlier than normal, catching me unawares. As she glided past me in the pool, I could see how Caitlin could be attracted to her muscular frame, manly bottom and firm breasts with dark areolas. I decided that I, too, would have her. As she coasted towards the shallow end, I stood in her swimming lane, my naked chest a firm cushion for her advancing head. She paused her stroke, her eyes showing no surprise as my naked body collided with hers. With a welcoming smile, she put her arms around my neck, shrugged off her thong and accepted my love making. Her shrieks of satisfied excitement echoed around the empty swimming pool arena when the coupling was completed. She floated backwards in the cooling water, her breasts cutting through the pool water like billowing sails on an ancient cutter.

"We shouldn't have done that," was all she said some minutes later. I just smiled, my body confidence somewhat restored and my mind cleared by this easy and pleasurable private retaliation.

Chapter 14

Remembering that encounter has given me an appetite. It must be time for my lunch. I may have reached my "dead-by date," but I can still enjoy lunch. Today, it is not to sustain me but simply for my pleasure. I wonder what Peter, my uncaring carer, will bring for me. Whilst I wait, let me tell you about how I and society were changing earlier this century and of some of the people I met at the hotels where Caitlin and I worked. Before then, I must tell you how the quiet young man I had met in Washington was becoming famous.

I first became aware of the rise in the Democratic Party in the US of the environmental and animal welfare campaigner, the charismatic young Jackson H James, when he stood for election. He was the man I knew and still think of as Hendrix. He reserved his middle name for friends when he was advised that the name Jackson would make him more electable. He is still Hendrix to me.

He was elected Senator for Massachusetts in the US mid-term elections on the retirement of eighty-four years old Edward Markey. The handsome forty years old Jackson Hendrix James, his beautiful wife Helen and two teenage children, epitomised the American dream. His message was clear. The transition to renewable energy and advances in carbon capture had not stopped rising temperatures. The US and the planet had to find another way.

The State of Massachusetts, the landing place of the Mayflower and the Pilgrims at the start of modern America, could and should again lead the way for a new beginning. Reducing animal farming and re-wilding the country would provide a natural carbon sink to help rebalance the atmosphere. It would allow the natural wildlife to flourish and avoid further soil erosion, river and sea pollution and mitigate the water shortages that were already causing deep concern.

Being elected by the US's most populated State was a start, but Hendrix's ambition remained frustrated. His environmental message received little support. The American people continued a diet heavy on meat that was causing endemic obesity and many associated illnesses. Little did I know then that the shy presidential aide, who put me up in his shabby bachelor flat that night in Washington, would one day become President of the US. The message he had learnt on his father-in-law's hog farm would change the world.

Chapter 15

Back to my story and to all the other people who shaped my education and turned me into the man I have become. Caitlin and I were always friends. She was a kind and intelligent woman and once her sexual frustrations were overcome, she blossomed. A happy Caitlin was the woman I had wanted to marry in public, and a contented lesbian in bed. Although I was always aware that she was sharing her bed with a lover, I enjoyed her financial protection, her company and the swagger that went with being her husband, at least in public. I understood her sexual confusion as it was an uncertainty that I shared. Maybe it was my hidden insecurities and distrust of being alone that kept me at her side and in her shadow. Maybe it was like living with my two sisters, cared for but always an outsider.

We had lots of celebrities staying at the Sandringham and I was always excited when members of the England football team stayed. The hotel had an exceptional gym and Spa facilities and was not too far from St George's Park, the Staffordshire home of the national team. We often found footballers staying for a few days during a break from training. The staff were all excited, none more than me, when superstar Olivia Goodstone came for a photo shoot.

I invited Josh because of his love for ladies' football. Caitlin was furious at this breach of hotel rules and I did understand Olivia's right to privacy, but Josh was my best friend and I knew he would be thrilled to meet Olivia Goodstone. In the event, he couldn't come and that was probably the best outcome.

Olivia had captained England and scored twice in the 2035 world cup final in US, beating the USA 4-2 on their home soil. At 23, Olivia was tall and athletic, with long golden hair. She looked wonderful in her tight England strip, a shirt that emphasised her small breasts, and tight shorts that displayed her long muscular legs. I felt an unusual lust for this wonderful example of a heroic woman. I imagined what it would be like to experience the strength and softness of her body. Memories of Aurora encouraged me to wonder if a well-exercised sinewy, lean female body was more sexy than the soft, delicate female form of my earlier dreams. I wanted to feel loved and excited by someone who would not let me down. It wasn't to be, as I discovered that evening.

I flirted with Olivia and she with me, as she sipped her mocktail at the bar before dinner. I remember that she wore an emerald-green body suit that stretched tightly over every part of her magnificent, sculptured body. Her very movement displayed a feral sexuality that fired my imagination. Caitlin joined us, I think initially to make sure my flirtation didn't go too far. Caitlin's fashionable elegance provided a sharp contrast to Olivia's untamed style, but immediately, there was a new dynamic. I was quickly forgotten. Olivia turned her attention to Caitlin who responded in a way only I could understand. I don't know which of them was first to suggest that they should inspect some hotel rooms together and I can only imagine their wild, ferocious sexuality together. Sitting at the bar alone I was jealous.

Even then Olivia also had a taste for young girls. Surrounded, as she was, by young fans, both male and female, she was too ready to give a cuddle as she posed for a selfie. On one occasion, I found her inviting two young girls to her room in the hotel. I had to interrupt to remind her that young visitors were not allowed in the bedrooms. I am glad that I did, in view of the scandals that would surround her later in life. She never visited the Sandringham again.

On another occasion, the Formula 1E commentator Lewis Hamilton stayed at the hotel. He had been a racing driver himself in the days of petrol-driven cars. He had adopted a vegan diet in 2017 to control his weight and improve energy levels but was now a passionate environmentalist. He used much of his considerable wealth and public platform to campaign to end animal farming. A small man, he was driven by his desire to find purpose alongside his love of motorsport and enabled by his wealth and celebrity. Over many dinners with Lewis, I learned a lot about the impact of animal farming on our environment.

Over 75% of the planet's farmland was devoted to farmed animals. Eating animals required a very inefficient use of land and water. If plants were used solely for human consumption, there would be plenty for all the world's population and many square miles of pastureland left for re-wilding. Deforestation and over-fertilisation were continuing in order to meet the demand for animal feed. If we could stop animal farming, heathland and forests would recover in just 20 years. Re-forestation would provide an extended habitat for the remaining species, many as yet undiscovered. The regrowth would create a carbon sink that could reverse global warming. The countryside would find its own balance of species. The world could recover its equilibrium naturally.

The overfishing in our seas had substantially depleted fish stocks that played an important role in carbon capture. By their lives, secretions and death, fish and sea mammals took carbon to the bottom of the oceans, trapping it indefinitely. Reduced fish stocks were already causing a depletion of the 31% of the carbon captured by our oceans and adding to the ever-rising global warming. An end to fishing would enable fish stock recovery and avoid the 640,000 tons of discarded fishing gear left in the ocean each year.

Lewis felt that he had enjoyed a very privileged life. He still had the benefit of stardom but not, it seemed, enough to convince others of what was so obvious to him. Despite his efforts, he could see little change.

I told him about my experiences with animal farming and the cruelty I had seen, but Lewis was not interested. He was only campaigning to eliminate greenhouse gasses and reduce our consumption of the limited resources on the planet. The impact of unsustainable and unnecessary animal agriculture in terms of land and water use and pollution could not continue unabated. It reminded me that we all see life from a different standpoint and look at issues from different directions. Sometimes, that does not stop us from seeing the same picture, albeit with the light falling in contrasting ways.

Chapter 16

I wonder how many hours of my life I have spent waiting for a meal. Where is Peter? With so little of my life left, I regret the hours I have wasted when I thought that I had all the time in the world. I must be patient. Let me tell you about Ireland, but please forgive me if I allow my meal to interrupt this conversation.

Away from the glamour of the Sandringham Hotel, Caitlin took me to Dublin to meet her family and help her celebrate the unification of Ireland. It had taken the failure of the power sharing government in Belfast and changes in the population demographics to effect change. It required two referendums in Southern Ireland before unification was accepted by a majority of the six million inhabitants of this beautiful, wet and windswept island. The conflict between Republicans and Unionists had been briefly re-ignited, but the secular population didn't have the passion of previous generations.

The desire for prosperity eventually held sway. An agreement was reached with the UK government after three years of wrangling about the share of the UK debt burden. Finally, on 1 November 2037, the island of Ireland became one country with a historic agreement signed by the President of Ireland, Leo Varadkar, Taoiseach Catherine Martin, and Prime Minister Jonathon Reynolds before the Irish Parliament in Leinster House. Residents of the old Northern Ireland reaped the benefits of full European Union membership and accepted the barrier to some trade with the UK that the Unionist parties had feared. The European Union border was secured and trade ambiguities had been resolved.

Although the economic consequences were not as positive as those promoted at the time, there were great expectations. I learned that nobody parties better than the Irish. We stayed in Caitlin's family's rambling Victorian home overlooking the beach in Dalkey, southeast Dublin. Her elderly parents were surprised and, I think, happy to see that their daughter had a husband at last. I played the part Caitlin wanted. Her family had arranged a party to celebrate Irelands unification and, belatedly, the marriage of their only daughter. I soon met with her 18 cousins with their husbands, wives and children for a huge party that filled the house with people, food, music and drinks. I loved the folk songs that came so quickly, although most were anti-British, and enjoyed the drunken choir's rendition of almost all of U2's back catalogue. It was the only time I saw Caitlin drop her guard and sing lustily, if rather tonelessly. The Irish were all happy when they arrived, happy whilst they were partying and happy when they left. Despite consuming huge quantities of alcohol, nobody sounded more inebriated leaving than they did arriving.

All of Caitlin's relatives wanted to know how we met and all about our brief romance and quick secret marriage. I was asked many times if Caitlin was pregnant in a guileless manner, which I at first found to be too direct, but I soon realised, reflected their uncomplicated view of life. Facing the reminder that there could be no children if I continued the current arrangements saddened me, but I decided to party for now and worry about children in the future. I didn't realise then how long the party would last.

There were too many guest names to remember and all with names too Irish to pronounce. I do remember Aoife. She wore a low-cut green dress that complimented her pale breasts, her silky red hair, her very white skin, her surprisingly blue eyes and her reckless tongue. She was an urgent conversationalist who spoke too quickly to allow interruption. Whilst I admired her open face and speculated about her ample hips, she told me that all her friends thought that Caitlin was gay. They didn't want to tell her conservative parents. I assured her that was not the case, keeping my fingers tightly crossed behind my back, as I had done when I told lies as a child.

Chapter 17

Peter has still not appeared. As this is to be my final day, I do think that the early glass of Merlot is appropriate. I can't resist the thought of popping a tomato and basil leaf on a crispy crouton into my rather dry mouth. I'll ask Peter to bring it for me. He's a nice robot with the predictability of automation, but I still resent having him share my house. I dislike arguing with a mechanical creature who always knows more than me. Thinking of the happiness that a glass of wine will bring reminds me of my guilty enjoyment of life during the MERS43 Pandemic in 2038.

The Sandringham was closed with just a skeleton maintenance staff during the MERS43 pandemic. This worldwide health crisis started in Wales, where chicken farm waste threatened the environmental balance. A vaccine based on the COVID scientific research was eventually produced and distributed, but not before one million deaths were recorded in the UK and more than a billion people died from the disease worldwide. The zoonotic transmitted virus was related to the Middle East Respiratory Syndrome. It had been transmitted from chickens to humans and then between humans. MERS43 had a very high fatality rate.

The River Wye was highly contaminated by an overload of phosphate in the water as heavy rain-washed livestock manure into the streams. The proliferation of huge chicken sheds in the catchment area had intensified the runoff and the warmer climate had encouraged the growth of algae that sucked out the oxygen, preventing all other life forms in the river. Higher levels of pneumonia and respiratory failure in the Wye Valley community were at first attributed to this environmental change and the warmer, humid climate. As a result, the local doctors were slow to diagnose the virus. The spike in deaths was recorded and, when the cause was identified, the world was warned and the UK was put in lockdown until a vaccine could be found.

Very soon, examples were discovered throughout the world. Isolation hospitals were quickly established and once again, the world's population was gripped in fear. When the source was exposed, UK hygiene standards were questioned. The examination of the chicken sheds only disclosed that all had met the then-current agricultural standards. With the inadequacy of those standards revealed and the unacceptable human health risks uncovered, the chicken and egg-producing companies would be forced into change.

In contrast to the COVID pandemic that had closed the economy in 2019, the government avoided daily reporting and imposed a blanket ban on reporting medical outcomes and deaths. The economy had not recovered sufficiently to afford a generous compensation package for those prevented from working by the shutdown and the only support given was an emergency food distribution. Hospitals were better prepared and the vaccine rollout was well-handled once the parameters of the disease had been established and means of immunisation designed and manufactured.

We were largely untouched by the illness at the Sandringham Hotel. We had little contact with the outside world once our guests left and our plant-based kitchen did not, of course, cook chicken or use eggs. I feel guilty for admitting that I enjoyed lockdown, although I was aware of the hardship suffered by so many families.

Caitlin had little to do with no guests to entertain but spent most of her time with her staff planning the return to work. Necessary maintenance and the installation of new flood protection kept her busy and engaged with the hotel. Often left alone, I maintained my routine of an hour in the gym each morning and 40 lengths of the pool before bed. I also started running again during the day. Away from the need to socialise with the hotel guests, I didn't eat rich food or drink alcohol. I lost a few pounds on my tummy and my skin glowed with good health.

On one sun-filled day in May, I had run for about five miles through the parkland when I stopped for a rest in the corner of a quiet, isolated field. I could feel the sun on my face and I took off my running shoes and then my shirt and shorts to catch the sun's warmth over my perspiring body. Lying on the dry grass and listening to the sounds of the marsh harrier, the bittern and the curlew in the still of the day, I felt totally at peace. My drowsing was interrupted by a gentle cough, and a flustered, rather embarrassed young hiker with long dark hair cascading over a white shirt and red shorts was standing in front of me saying, "Can I join you?". I quickly pulled on my shorts, any thoughts of the restrictions on human interaction quickly forgotten. The confident young stranger kicked off her walking boots, sat beside me unasked and explained that she was a third-year university student about to sit her finals. She was taking a walk to clear her head before the exam.

She told me that she needed something to take her mind off the exam and had I any ideas. I asked her what she would like to do, and she blushed when she said, "We should make love and live happily ever after with a very special memory." I had always dreamed of meeting a beautiful princess in a field of golden corn blowing in the wind and this was as near as I would ever get. My own body was already aroused by the feel of the sun and the excitement and risk of the outdoors. I looked at her soft, young body as she unbuttoned her shirt to reveal bronzed naked breasts. When she slid out of her red shorts and removed a matching thong, I almost ejaculated in my own running shorts. We didn't exchange names, hardly spoke at all, but made love excitedly, vigorously and noisily until I dozed off to sleep, spent and satisfied.

When I woke, there was no sign of my young lover, and I was left wondering if it had all been a dream enhanced by my own well-practiced fingers. Maybe she had to rush back for her exam. Maybe she didn't exist at all.

I ran through that field at the same time every day for two

weeks. I just wanted to know how she had scored in her exams, or that is what I told myself. I never saw her again, but she left me with a happy memory that I share with you today. I hope that if she was ever real and is still alive, that she too, will remember meeting a naked runner in a field

October 2038 COP 44 Krakow Poland

COP 44 was a virtual event hosted by the Polish city of Krakow.

The rise in global temperatures to 1.9 above pre-industrial levels had long surpassed the tipping point for climate change. Ocean levels had risen 45 cm since the turn of the century. The world population had grown to 9 billion. Awareness was growing as so many countries had been ravaged by severe weather events, raging bush fires and devastating floods. Reduction in the use of fossil fuels had not yet halted the growth of greenhouse gasses.

Chapter 18

The predictable Peter has served my lunch. We often get asked what we would choose for a final meal but now, faced with the choice in reality, I find that I have little appetite. My wish for tomato and basil had passed, so I asked for a ripe avocado. So few are grown now with the water shortage and Peter couldn't find one. As my starter course I am given a second crop of asparagus from my garden with a dressing of Olive Oil from the local olive tree orchard.

Peter has prepared a full roast dinner with roast potatoes, carrots, peas, sage and onion stuffing, apple sauce and Yorkshire pudding. He has not forgotten my favourite vegan gravy and a taste of mustard. It is very annoying Peter that never forgets anything. A good roast dinner never needed the meat my parents used to eat because the taste is largely in the vegetables, gravy and sauces. I might not finish it all. I hope that Peter has brought the glass of Merlot for me. I will have to keep recording whilst I eat as I still have much to explain. Another orange from the garden, peeled and quartered, sits on a plain white plate as I continue.

I was still ridiculously hopeful about my situation with Caitlin. I really wanted a loving relationship, a son and a proper family. My dreams were overtaken by international travel and the chance to experience another country. Of course, another lady then entered my life.

It was a shock when Caitlin was called to manage Jin Jiang's flagship hotel in Shanghai. The Jin Jiang Hotel was to celebrate a centenary of trading in September 2040. The Board felt that Caitlin was best able to attract the most international celebrities as guests for the celebrations. She took chef Aurora with her to manage the restaurants and I followed a month later, when a new manager, George Tanner, and his wife arrived at the Sandringham Hotel.

After the extensive gardens and parkland of the Sandringham Estate I found the crowded streets of Shanghai very challenging. My lack of Chinese vocabulary prevented me from enjoying the local community and initially, I was unhappy. The climate was cold and damp when I arrived but my disappointments were nothing compared to the distress during the hot, humid, summer conditions

I stayed mostly in the central area of this large sprawling city of 25 million people wandering around between the towering skyscrapers and many renovated heritage buildings as I tried to escape the busy hotel. I couldn't settle in this gateway between East and West, the financial centre of China but I was soon introduced to the dwindling ex-pat community and found a company in my new friend, Madison, who had been in the city for 15 years and was saddened by the changes that political isolation had brought.

Madison helped me fill my days in Shanghai. In the evenings I played the role of hotel host that I had mastered at the Sandringham. Caitlin was busy in the day and Madison helped me sightsee around this busy city. Tall with blonde hair and the palest blue eyes I had ever seen, Madison was almost always dressed in a T-shirt, washed blue jeans and white trainers. Her pale complexion, emphasised by her hair, stood out in the crowded streets. Her vitality was not yet dulled by her experience of Shanghai. She was very aware of the city and seemed delighted to inform me. I was thrilled to be a student of her knowledge.

We walked together along the Bund, Shanghai's promenade on the west bank of the Huangpujiang River, where the city had a European feel. The many English and French buildings stood elegantly, refusing to be part of the city bustle below them. We arrived at Huangpu Park. Madison took me to see the statues of the Jade Buddha Temple and the amazing Hall of the Kings of Heaven. The splendour of the ornate structures was only a stage set for the statues of the Four Kings of Heaven that dominated the space. We visited the old town, where the sixteenth-century buildings provided a more exotic feel. It was in the Garden of Happiness, to the northeast of the town, where I told Madison how happy she made me feel. From then on it was like a secret holiday romance. I felt no guilt towards Caitlin and Madison was, I thought, free of any relationship. We both lived in the moment. I had not yet learnt that every relationship brings its own complications.

After only a few days of sightseeing, wandering together, sharing our opinions and giggling at the absurdities of life, we found ourselves chasing a street kiss into Madison's apartment. There we found a stillness that was a deep contrast to the passion of our lovemaking. Like me, Madison had a huge amount of love hibernating in her body. She released her passion with a fervour I had not experienced before. Soon our sightseeing was mostly from her bedroom window. It was in this bed that Madison gave me the silver forever love bracelet with its Chinese writing and half dragon's head that was to cause so much trouble. However, the idyllic adventure eventually turned into a nightmare, but not before Madison had described the impossible city of Shanghai and the complications of life in China to me as we lay nestled together in air-conditioned comfort and post-coital devotion, listening to the recorded sounds of George Strait singing his country and western hit Pure Country over and over again.

Shanghai was a vast city of 35 million people. They had suffered slow economic growth during the COVID lockdown periods of 20 years ago and never recovered vibrancy. Memories of the lockdown had influenced the response to the MERS43 pandemic. The more liberal policy adopted in 2038 had resulted in many more deaths. Every family had experienced loss and the population focused their anger on the politicians. The crowded streets were no longer carrying the fashionably dressed international businessmen and financiers that had delivered the rapid growth of the early century. Following the exclusion from many international markets, Chinese political leaders had tried to create the consumer economy needed to sustain industrial production. The Chinese were still sceptical of home manufactured goods and the economy had stalled. A four-day working week and insufficient income to enjoy the limited entertainment available, left most workers frustrated and with time on their hands. Already rising temperatures were amplifying heat stress and the poor government response to the increasing number of typhoons, floods and snow events highlighted administrative shortfalls. Rising sea levels presented an ever-present threat to a billion people in precarious coastal locations already enduring storm surges and heavy rain storms.

This was a time of political uncertainty in China. Xi Jinping had resigned as General Secretary in 2025 after the COVID crisis riots forced the end of the Zero COVID policy. The sixty-one years old Hu Chunhua had been reinstated to the Politburo and made the youngest-ever General Secretary of the Communist Party. His 10 years of continued repression and authoritarian control as economic growth slowed, fuelling opposition. The changes he had made to enable the resumption of international trade had introduced the Western ideas he sought to discourage and the ideological ideas he feared. Foreign travel had introduced a celebrity culture and with it, a demand for younger leadership, chosen democratically. Young people wanted greater freedoms and the Central Committee of the Chinese Communist Party had appointed Fenhua Li as General Secretary to respond to the clamour for change.

Fenhua Li was a reformer. She had outlawed mass arbitrary detention without access to legal counsel and released what were described as political agitators. She closed the internment camps that had been unsuccessfully used to eradicate ethnic, cultural and religious beliefs. She cancelled policies of involuntary birth control and forced sterilisation and outlawed forced marriage. Fenhua allowed religious freedom and the observation of previously banned religious practices but did not allow access to international social media or the general freedom of expression. These new freedoms only resulted in the demand for more and the further clamour for change.

In the luxury hotel surroundings, only a mile from the city centre, it felt as though we were in the calm middle of a brewing storm and so it proved. And the storm would bring my relationship with Madison to an embarrassing end.

I had been enjoying Madison's affection only in the afternoons because I had hotel hosting duties in the evenings. Unknown to me, Madison carried out her own hosting activities in the evenings. Her nighttime companion was Feng Hong, a leading member of the Communist Party, Mayor of Shanghai. His patronage had been paying for the smart apartment and cooling air conditioning I had so much enjoyed. I imagine that it was his understanding of the political situation that Madison had been explaining to me.

When Madison and Feng Hong arrived together at the Jin Jiang Hotel for a state dinner, their first sight was my performance of being a loving husband to Caitlin. Madison was acting as the perfect partner to the diminutive Chinese politician.

Feng Hong was wearing a silver cuff bracelet identical to mine. When he saw that the half-dragon's head on my bracelet was the opposite twin to his own, he realised that Madison had passed his love token to me. The furious senior official, trying to save face, stamped off angrily, his features rumbling like thunder. Madison and I couldn't stop giggling, so much so that our deceit was exposed. Madison would learn that Chinese men cannot tolerate being ridiculed. To my disappointment I learnt that Caitlin didn't care, so long as it was kept private. Feng Hong abandoned Madison and she returned to the UK. It was to be many years before I would see Madison again. I would have faced the prospect of being treated as a spy if Feng Hong had not been too embarrassed to make the situation public. Fortunately the threats to have my visa withdrawn disappeared in the political upheaval that was to follow.

On 4 July 2039, the streets of Shanghai filled with what was estimated to be eight million souls in a coordinated campaign march that was mirrored throughout the country. Half a billion people throughout China demanded democratic government. The communist party conceded control. A bloodless change of power led to acceptance by

America and the West, the resumption of trade agreements and eventually the restoration of economic success for the hardworking Chinese people. China would celebrate Independence Day with America, Washington with Beijing, and New York with Shanghai.

The Jin Jiang Hotel became the centre of that busy time as world business leaders and politicians gathered to play their part in the transformation and to grasp whatever share of the financial fallout they could. I became a disregarded presence in the hotel as I performed my hosting duties, quietly observing the discussions as I rearranged the floral displays, collected the used brandy glasses or folded the complimentary newspapers. Caitlin and I realised huge profits from the investment tips I overheard from informed guests as the Shanghai stock exchange boomed and then enjoyed a period of frightening volatility. I would meet Madison again, but not for some years.

Fenhua Li was eventually re-elected as the President with a huge majority for her democratic communist party.

Chapter 19

My lunch is over. I enjoyed the Merlot, and demanded another glass but Peter refused to get me one and I don't know where he hides the bottles. I regret informing him of my heart condition and having Peter programmed to control my diet. It doesn't seem important now. He should have been reprogrammed. I spent too long re-living my time in Shanghai to enjoy the lunch, but my brief affair with Madison is a happy memory. Not so happy is my memory of the Jakarta disaster. The major tragedy occurred in 2039 and, although I didn't witness it, I felt close to the action because The President of Indonesia, Megawati Suharto, was staying at the Jin Jiang Hotel when she first heard of the terrible loss of life.

Megawati Suharto was in Shanghai leading a trade mission to China when the devastating news came through. The sea defences had been expanded after the 2021 floods that brought three-metre floods to part of the city, but a fifteen-metre sea surge, during high winds and torrential rain, had breached these sea defences and raced into the city. The surge destroyed all before it. The city of twelve million people, on the crowded Java Island, had been sinking at 10 centimetres each year. More than half the city was four metres below sea level. Over two million lives were lost and the city was destroyed. The four metres high flood waters could not be pumped away. The flood walls were beyond repair. A city of twelve million people was lost forever. Indonesia had moved the capital city administration to the new city of Nusantara, built in Borneo, 2000 miles away in 2026, but only the political elite had moved. Jakarta had remained the commercial and cultural centre of the region. Slowing worldwide economic growth during the 2030's had prevented the necessary investment in sea defences. The changes in weather patterns caused by global warming had destroyed many lives.

Megawati was in tears for her fellow citizens at this calamity. It was to end her political ambitions and leave a scar on the world that is still remembered. I found her crying, alone in the hotel's library and I too felt overwhelmed by the scale of the losses. I tried to comfort her. I told her that Indonesia needed her strength to overcome the tragedy and to rebuild the nation's confidence. She knew that there were more problems to come as the sea level rises continued. Her nation of islands was so vulnerable. I could not find the words to reassure her. The world's leaders still refused to acknowledge the size of the crisis for so many island nations. I believed then that only a real catastrophe in America would persuade the wealthy nations to take note and make the essential changes. This was to be the case, but I didn't know then that Jackson Hendrix James would become the 49th President of the US.

Chapter 20

I think of my life ending after 88 years of experience and the wisdom it has brought me. I can't help an enormous sadness at the thought of all the people, some of them friends and family, who have lost their lives at a much younger age. Each one of us brings something to the human experience. We all do acts of kindness and regret our acts of selfishness. All around the world, there is unnecessary death. Now I imagine those dead people enjoying country walks, family gatherings, successes and failures. And I can't ignore the many billions of farmed animals that have been used for food who also deserve a life. I think of excess for some and starvation for others because of the selfish food choices we have made. I regret the loss of habitat for so many sentient creatures. So many lives have been taken by our food choices, pandemics and the consequences of man-made climate change. All this destruction is caused by the impact generations before us unknowingly imposed on our climate. I haven't the time to ponder over the lives lost, so onward with a more optimistic story, or is it?

It wasn't all disappointment at the Jin Jiang Hotel. The centenary celebration dinner was a great success. The vaccination programme for MERS 43 had enabled the return of travel and the democratisation of China had caused a new rapport with America. Caitlin had been like a bear with a sore head for weeks as she prepared for the banquet that was attended by President Fenhua Li and the whole Jin Jiang Board of Directors. With senior politicians from all around the world still chasing the opportunities to sell to the second largest single population in the world after India, there was no shortage of takers for the event. I was seated between recently elected UK Conservative Prime Minister Justin Macmillan and deputy head of NATO the Canadian Rolf Peters.

Justin Macmillan had been elected on a small majority after 15 years of a Labour government. The changing population demographics and heavy debt had put public services under pressure. The Nation's Debt had soared to unsustainable levels. At first, the Reynolds government policies seemed sensible. The reduction in the Civil Service brought about by the simplification of taxes was resisted by the Unions until very favourable redundancy terms were agreed. After years of wrangling the staff reductions were achieved but the burden of extra civil service pensions and job seekers allowance surpassed the salary savings. The new car tax system Prime Minister Jonathon Reynolds had introduced, encouraged the sale of electric vehicles and a vast reduction in petrol car miles causing a substantial fall in government revenue once the initial car sales tax had been paid. National Health Service costs were spiralling out of control despite reducing demand. The electorate called for better fiscal management, but I doubted whether the new Prime Minister, Justin Macmillan MP was the man for the job. I estimated that he would abandon the essential environmental policies to deliver the needed economic recovery.

At the celebration dinner, Caitlin had arranged my seating to keep Rolf Peters from discussing the UK's failure to meet its military contribution to NATO with Justin Macmillan. I talked about my idea for euthanasia for the elderly as small talk, to avert more controversial subjects. I suggested that everybody over 80 years old should be assessed and, if appropriate, be the subject to enforced assisted dying at the biological age of 80. This would encourage healthy lifestyles that would delay death, ensure that the health services would not be overwhelmed by bed blocking and give fellow citizens the certainty of a painless death without being a burden on society or their families. We could all expect to die without losing our dignity. The state would enjoy substantial savings in medical care and state pension provision. Private pension arrangements would be simplified by the life time certainty and nobody would spend their last days watching their savings diminish to give them a painful and hopeless life.

Both politely listened to me making controversial dinner talk to avoid more serious debate. Little did I think that my ideas would be approved by the House of Commons, only three years later. I never realised that I would now be a victim of this policy. Justin Macmillan really wanted to talk about football and his appointment of Olivia Newstone as his Minister for Sport, now that she had given up football. I could only guess his real intentions for a closer relationship with the overtly sexy ex-footballer but felt sure that he would be disappointed.

Rolf Peters could only mutter about the lack of military support for NATO and the continuing crisis in the Middle East to anybody who would listen. I was his only audience because the Chinese minister for Defence, sitting on his right, spoke no English and Rolf spoke no Chinese. I chose not to act as an interpreter. I politely listened as he explained that a new religious tolerance between Sunni and Shia Muslims had eased some of the tension in the Middle East. The fall in oil demand had reduced prices and volumes of pumped barrels. This had exposed some unexpected debts. The changing climate was impacting scarce water supplies. With oil revenues in decline, Saudi Arabia had withdrawn support for Palestine's continuing conflict with Israel but, without intervention from America, there would be no peace settlement to a war that had not been resolved ever since the Zionist occupation almost 100 years ago. Rolf hoped that the centenary of the Jewish state in 2048 would create that opportunity and we contemplated that the Jin Jiang Hotel was older than the state of Israel. I didn't know then that I would be in Jerusalem to see the culmination of peace talks.

Chapter 21

When I was working in Shanghai, the hotel paid for my many flights back to London. I was usually accompanied by Caitlin. The twelve-hours flights gave me the space to think. I started to worry about the future. Was my constant air travel justified? Something had to change to save the planet because intense weather events were becoming commonplace. I had no children, or so I thought, but felt a heavy concern for the generations to follow. Global warming, rising sea levels, overfishing and sea and river pollution continued unabated. Could I make a change?

Caitlin and I had returned to London for my fortieth birthday. I had not visited my family since I had married Caitlin, perhaps because I didn't want to lie to them. I felt ashamed that I had continued this pretend marriage, aware every night, that I was alone whilst Caitlin was sleeping with her lover in the next room. I had, of course, kept in touch with my parents and my younger sisters, speaking to them as often as I could. I used my travels as an excuse for not going home. I also feared that my father would not like Caitlin, but I needn't have worried. When I arrived at our family home in the Surrey Hills my parents gave Caitlin the full British welcome. My father's oversized gin and tonic ensured that the feast of curried aubergine with bell peppers, tomatoes, and rice would not be remembered.

When my father told me that I was still his favourite child, I remember that he had always told all three of us that we were his favourite. He used to hand out our monthly pocket money when we were children claiming that his pay packet was "A bit low this month" and one of us would have to go without. If we were the unlucky one, we should not complain, or gloat if we had received our money. We had to look after each other because one of us had no money. Of course, it didn't take us long to discover that we all received the payout.

My sisters were both at home for my visit and as we enjoyed our laughter and reminiscences, they showed me photographs of their children. Wishing to avoid the reminder that I was childless and sensing that Caitlin felt comfortable in this easy home I sat with my dad as we talked together over a glass of Cognac.

My father had spent most of his working life on the railways after his banking experience had end abruptly when I was a child. Now he had been made redundant. It was four years before his state pension would be paid when he reached 70. The Union had arranged attractive terms and he would not be short of money but he was devastated at the total closure of the railway network. The government had announced the phased closure of all railway lines to make way for the new Cascadeways that would carry the electric driverless convey cars and super conveycoaches on intercity journeys. 120,000 employees would lose their jobs and 10,000 miles of rail track would be taken up. The Cascadeways would provide the automatic in-journey battery charging needed for longer journeys at a much lower cost than the £30 billion spent each year on subsidies for the railways.

I felt sorry for Dad and his colleagues who would have to find new employment but realised that this was a brave and positive move by Justin Macmillan's government. Perhaps he wasn't the lightweight I had assumed. Taking on the Rail Workers Union was a big challenge for any government, but I imagine that the Union had to accept the reality of change in the end.

On the way back to our hotel Caitlin and I were caught up in the 10th annual Animal Troops for Freedom March. Over a million people, all dressed in brightly coloured boiler suits with different animal head masks representing both farm and wild animals, marched from Hyde Park Corner, down Piccadilly across to Trafalgar Square and onto Downing Street to deliver a clear message to ban animal farming. The pandemic had ruined confidence in chicken farming and exposed the dangers of crowded agricultural sheds, but the Government still disregarded the cruelty, pollution, environmental damage and the wastefulness of a system that seemed too ingrained in society to change. The government had not yet banned factory farming and slaughterhouses.

The march ended peacefully with a party back in Hyde Park. Caitlin and I joined the hopeful celebration. On a big stage set up in Hyde Park, pop band Pigsica, dressed in rainbow-coloured boiler suits and animal heads, played in front of a huge screen showing the conditions in factory farms, conditions that met government standards but imposed extensive cruelty on farmed animals. The crowd was incensed and an emotional Caitlin shared my tears. Surely the government could not ignore the brutality displayed on the screens or disregard this well-humoured protest. The government seemed to be in the pocket of the big investors in animal farming. Looking back, I can't really understand how we thought that animal flesh was a necessary part of our diet or that we could treat the affectionate chickens, cows and pigs as commodities to be eaten when now they bring so much joy to families. I imagine that these loving creatures were tricked into being a food source many years ago because they were so happy to be domesticated. After all humans never tried to enslave lions for food.

Chapter 22

I have still not heard from my hoped-for guest. He has never been good at responding to my invitations, but surely this one last request won't be refused. What will I say to him? What will he think of me and my selfish wish to record this account of my life and the twenty-first century? Will he even listen? Maybe he will be interested in Madison, I certainly was.

It was a bit of a shock when I saw Madison again. She hadn't changed from our assignations in Shanghai. She was at the Animal Troops for Freedom march, looking great in her pale green boiler suit with pretend rabbit ears perched against her blonde hair as she danced along to Pigsica with the energy I remembered being directed in another way. She didn't spot me in the crowd, but I couldn't keep my eyes away from her as she appeared at last to have found her purpose in life. Her action for animals was clearly bringing its own rewards, as I could see from her obvious popularity amongst her fellow activists. If anybody could make it fun to be campaigning against cruelty, it was Madison. It was Madison who shared with me one of my most upsetting experiences and one of the funniest, all at the same time.

Some weeks after seeing Madison I found her contact details on the Animal Troops campaign WEB page and contacted her to congratulate her on her dancing at the Animal Troops for Freedom March. During a rather awkward telephone conversation, Madison invited me to join her in a vigil at the slaughterhouse in Northern Ireland where one thousand six months old pigs were killed every hour.

I jumped at the chance to meet Madison again and to escape the weather in Shanghai. I told myself that I went to Ireland because I loved the people and because of my curiosity to understand what had motivated the change in Madison. I just fancied Madison and wanted to restart our arrangement. That wasn't to be, but my visit was life changing experience. I wish that I could forget my first and only visit to a slaughterhouse.

The sights, sounds and smells of the needless life destruction of the abattoir have never left me. Writing this, the dreadful images of the scale of killing are floating back. I am gagging for breath as I remember the taste, aroma and noise of death.

Despite changing eating habits, the UK was slaughtering more than a billion land animals each year, almost all from mega-farms. Ireland with its access to the European Union markets was a leading producer. Many of the animals finished up in this massive facility to end their captive lives in tortured misery.

I met Madison and her fervent friends on the overnight ferry from Liverpool to Belfast. They explained the major moves to a plant-based diet that had been achieved in the United Kingdom. They celebrated the part played by activists throughout the century. However, there was still a worldwide demand for pork products. The north of Ireland was home to continuing intensive pig farms. The slaughterhouse that we were to visit was one of the few remaining fully active.

The presence of our band of volunteer activists with our simple banners was designed to prick the conscience of slaughterhouse workers, suppliers and customers. To give focus to the demonstration there was to be a performance of the visual representation of humans being treated in the same way as pigs in an art installation designed by Stephanie Lane in collaboration with Susan Clarke. This was part of the efforts to rid the world of speciesism and to recognise the rights of all species. The work of the activists would be escalated by the mushrooming expansion of social media.

A reporter on the Irish News, who supported the cause, had promised local media coverage but it was unlikely that we could achieve national publicity. That was not to be the outcome.

There was a dozen of us who arrived at the Belfast Docks and joined a small coach for the one-hour journey to the abattoir. The drive passing Lough Neagh was beautiful and we all remarked on the wonders of the natural world before we entered the contrasting complex of industrial units that made up the slaughterhouse.

This pig-killing factory, described as a harvesting process facility in the company literature, was state of the art, government approved and supported by the animal protection agent, the RSPCA, who gave their stamp of approval in return for financial contributions. The protesters proclaimed that killing could never be considered humane.

The gates to the industrial complex were firmly shut to us as we stood outside on a warming but breezy Wednesday morning. Even here, outside the facility, the air was thick with the odour of death and was polluted by the smell of unintended pig faeces that fell from the incoming lorries with their doomed victims. There was a constant flow of wagons holding hundreds of squalling pigs, unhappy with the crowded, cramped and congested transport conditions but still unaware of the fate that waited for them.

Suddenly, as a truck passed through the gate, it made a jolt forward, struck the gate's substantial post at speed and slipped on its side. The six-month-old pigs fattened to the one-hundren-and- twenty-kilogram slaughter weight, bundled themselves from the sides of the stricken lorry and chortled off into the neighbourhood. As the security men rushed to capture the squealing escapees the activists scurried past the gates carrying me with them. Once inside it was easy to enter the killing lines through unlocked doors.

Pigs brought to the slaughterhouse were given twelve hours in a holding area before being taken for slaughter. Ten thousand pigs, unfed from before their transport, were packed into several enormous, overcrowded pens where they were hosed down and left to await their fate. The smell of pigs' blood mixed with their faeces that had fallen through the slatted floor of the pens was overwhelming.

The pens of pigs were delivered to the stunning chambers in the strict order of their arrival. They were roughly herded into a smaller pen for 50 pigs. This was then loaded down into the gas chamber. Crowded on top of each other, the pigs struggled to breathe, forcing their snouts up against the ceiling of the chamber as the heavy carbon dioxide was pumped into it. We heard the snorts and screams of the pigs as they struggled to survive in a hopeless battle for life. For two and a half minutes of intense fear and pain, the gas burnt the pigs from the inside ending consciousness. The gas chamber wall opened and the desecrated carcasses were tipped into the butchering section.

The stunned animals were taken and hung by one leg on a moving wrack. Their throats were sliced open by the slaughter man's knife and blood poured from them to mix with their predecessors in huge pools on the floor. Not all the pigs were completely stunned and those that felt lucky to find a gap in the ceiling of the gas chamber to avoid the full effects of the CO2 now realised that the luck they had celebrated was bad luck. These pigs could see what horror had fallen on their companions. Their resistance was hopeless and their twisting and turning made no difference to the slaughter man's knife. As I watched, horrified by the endless line of carcasses moved to the butchering area, Madison shouted for my help.

With security still distracted, the activists decided to release the pigs in the holding pens. The shed gates were thrown open as we all rushed round to usher the still reluctant pigs from their pens to the outside world.

I don't know whether a pig can show happiness in the face, but I like to think that they were all amused to see the continuing bedlam outside the industrial complex as the pigs we rescued met with the earlier escapees. Even their Irish wardens had to smile at the ridiculous bedlam that ensued before they aborted their attempts to return the escapees to their harrowing deaths.

We escaped too, quickly back for the overnight ferry back to Liverpool after a successful day, albeit with horrifying memories of the scale of the torture and the thoughtless cruelty. I don't know what happened to the pigs that escaped but their excitement and confusion to be in the open-air stays with me today.

Madison had never expected the international media coverage. The Irish Times reporter who had reluctantly covered the rather boring vigil had an international scoop. His video of the carnage outside the slaughterhouse as the photogenic pigs made fools of the potbellied security staff, was covered on mainstream news channels throughout the world. It earned him a fortune and gave him new respect for the pigs. Our footage of the inside of the abattoir received over two million views and helped to persuade viewers that a bacon sandwich was not worth the pain it caused. I was never to see Madison again.

Chapter 23

I fear that nobody will turn up for my final night. I only want one person. Most of my friends have already passed. I will ask Peter to join me. He might learn something. He might even have his own suggestions for my story. Perhaps Peter will give me some credit when I have gone. Perhaps my garden here will be left to go wild now that I will not be around to give it the love it deserves. I was a proud first contributor to the world's earliest national rewilding project. Let me tell you how I got involved in the Planet for Pleasure Initiative.

I was on another short break in London again to see family and friends when Prince George, Duke of Wales, announced his "Planet for Pleasure Initiative" to celebrate his thirty-first birthday. The decline in demand for milk, due to probiotic milk and the popularity of other plant-based milks, had closed many small farms and left farming families with uncertain futures.

The growth in vertical farming, where vegetables and grains are grown close to the markets in huge high-rise buildings, was proving commercially successful. The careful control of the water, light and nutrients required to produce and nurture plants was a high-tech activity best achieved inside buildings.

Agricultural land values for pastureland had collapsed. This Planet for Pleasure Initiative had royal approval, government and private funding, and National Trust support and intended to create popular membership. The funds raised would enable the acquisition and maintenance of vast areas of inexpensive farmland to create new re-wilded leisure areas for walking, cycling, outdoor swimming, bird watching and the observation of natural wildlife.

The farmers, funded by farm subsidies, would act as wardens, supervising the land they knew so well. By allowing these wild areas the "Planet for Pleasure Initiative" would provide work for the farming community, recreation for the local population, wildlife habitat and a carbon sink to allow the planet to repair itself. The undrained wetlands would re-appear to hold flood waters and slow river flows to reduce flooding. The trees would provide oxygen, store carbon and stabilise the soil.

Eventually nature would find its own balance and the animal population would be self-regulating. The charity would start with the transfer of fifty thousand hectares of land owned by the Duchy of Cornwall, in the gift of Prince George. The charity planned to control a million hectares of re-wilded land by 2050, approximately a quarter of the UK farmland not suitable for crops but, until now, denuded of wildlife by the use as pasture.

I was among the first to sign up for my annual membership in a scheme that would prove to be a blueprint for change that travelled the world. This initiative alone, ensured Prince George's place in the history of our planet.

Chapter 24

It's probably a good thing that Peter wouldn't serve me the extra glass of Merlot because the lunchtime wine has made me sleepy. I must resist the drowsiness if I am to complete my story and persuade you, and myself, that my life hasn't been wasted. I guess that we all want to leave our mark, even when we realise how quickly the deceased are forgotten. Back to my story and my second stay in Washington DC.

It was a strange coincidence that Caitlin was asked to manage the opening of the refurbished New Willard Hotel in Washington. We moved there in August 2043. Caitlin brought her chef, Aurora, with her and they started establishing the reputation of the vegan restaurant whilst my presence hid the reality of their personal life. I was at ease in the luxury surroundings and my interest in politics was rewarded with lots of conversations with aides and candidates who sought out my information and local gossip.

Jackson Hendrix James recognised me as soon as he entered the hotel. It had been 20 years since our brief meeting. Hendrix had put on a little weight and there was a hint of grey in his unruly hair. He had replaced the steel rimmed spectacles I remembered with eye correction, but was easily recognisable from the posters that announced his candidacy for President. Although I couldn't help thinking of him as Hendrix, he had dropped the name in favour of the more campaign suitable Jackson. Hendrix had preserved the appearance of an academic man, more interested in listening than talking. He had a sparkle in his clear blue eyes that suggested humour rather than danger. This did not conceal his reassuring frame and casual good looks. I could see how the young girls would see him as protector, whilst older women would want to mother him. His determination was matched by a hint of vulnerability that made him approachable.

Although Hendrix was tall and still slim, his well-tailored suits still carried the crumpled style of a man in a hurry, a man who didn't have time to worry about his appearance. Since the television age, the US electors have placed the appearance of the candidates before policy and performance. I worried that Jackson Hendrix James didn't follow the trend.

I was arranging flowers in the reception hall when Hendrix approached me to say he remembered our evening together and that it had helped him decide his future. He asked if we could get together again.

Over the next few months, Hendrix stayed at the New Willard when he was in Washington and we often had supper together. We became good friends and when he was off campaigning, I missed his company. I found myself awaiting his return with eager anticipation. For almost 18 months he stayed at the New Willard whenever his campaign trail allowed and more frequently than he should.

We discussed the May 2044 re-election of Justin Macmillan's conservative party in the UK. Macmillan had increased his majority in the House of Commons whilst promoting environmental policies that included the abolition of animal farming subsidies in favour of subsidies for the maintenance of re-wilding projects and the encouragement of a plant-based diet. Hendrix felt that a similar policy in the US would be a vote loser and that, without power, he would have little chance of achieving the results he wanted. His team calculated that the big increase in State Pensions funded by a withdrawal from nuclear weapon development were the measures that had secured the Macmillan re-election.

We only really discussed possible vote-winning policies and I began to question whether Hendrix's ethical stand on factory farming had deserted him. I needn't have worried. All he wanted to talk about was his campaign and to test his ideas. He never really mentioned his wife Helen, but he did tell me that her mother had died in the MERS 43 pandemic and that her father, Nathan, had committed suicide shortly afterwards.

Helen had inherited the farm, stopped livestock farming and converted the pig sheds into giant indoor vegetable growing facilities. I noted that Helen did not accompany him on the campaign trail, but I said nothing. If Jackson wanted to talk about her, it was for him to raise the subject. I supposed Helen was busy with the farm. Jackson did worry that his two children would be brought into the media spotlight if he was made President, but they were now in their twenties and he thought they could handle it.

Hendrix expressed self-doubt about the size of his responsibilities if he won. I reassured him that he would win to be the 49th President of The United States of America, and I often called him Mr President, although he feared that this anticipation might bring him bad luck. I knew that he would carry those responsibilities better than anybody else. We talked about what he could achieve, and he told me how much my kindness was helping him. He said that I had been kind to offer a sympathetic ear all those years ago and was being kind now to provide an understanding sounding board without asking any questions or wanting anything in return. If only the whole of America could be so kind to each other life would be so much better.

I like to think that those long conversations we had together helped shape his Presidency with the worldwide impact it had, but nobody even knew my name.

I remember how undeservedly proud I felt at the Inaugural Address given by President Jackson James on his taking Office on 20th of January 2045. I also felt sorry that my time with him had come to an end. His change of name seemed to signify that our friendship was over. I was in the crowd there to hear his speech given on the ceremonial porch of the Capitol Building and to a worldwide television audience of millions. I couldn't confess to my part in its construction, but

I kept a copy.

"My fellow citizens have elected me with a clear mandate to make America kind again. With overwhelming majorities in the House and the Senate, we recognise the demand for the radical change that we will deliver. Our citizens demand a change from greed to sharing, from cruelty to compassion, from fear to hope. Our citizens demand we act for them and are not driven by the big business lobby, the rich and famous, the few who fund our campaigns and put profit before compassion. For us all and by us all, we will make America kind again.

When our founders settled in Jamestown Virginia in 1607 they were strong men, but they were kind. Neighbour helped neighbour, Protestant helped Catholic, Catholic helped Jew. America was a place of refuge for those who sought escape from bigotry and found kindness on these shores. English, Irish, French, Dutch, Swedes and Spanish all helped each other. There was help, not resentment, support not opposition and unity not division as these men created our great country. Now, as we also face immense challenges, we need America to be kind again, to be compassionate again, to be honest again, to support each other. We must remind ourselves that it's better to give than to receive, to praise than to criticise, to conserve than to destroy.

We need to stop the gun culture that should not define us. There have been two mass shootings every day for the last 25 years, more than 65000 unnecessary and unwanted deaths. There are half a billion guns in private hands in America, half the guns in the world, and a culture of aggression that goes with them. We must bring this to a stop. When the 32nd President, Franklin D Roosevelt, gave his State of the Union Address to this House, 104 years ago, he defined the four freedoms demanded for any civilised society; freedom of speech, freedom of religion, freedom from want and freedom from fear. Fear has returned to our society and I demand of all my fellow citizens, that we banish fear.

In my first act as President will be to ban the carrying of firearms outside the home without a licence. Licences will only be issued to properly qualified police officers, training service personnel and authorised and approved gun clubs. The reward for the success of this policy will be an end to the mass shootings that have dogged this country for almost a century, citizens who will not fear for their lives, and children who can go to school without worry...

Changing gun culture alone will help make America kind again but we need to do more than that. We need communities to support each other and businesses that bolster the communities that provide their workforce. I will reduce by one percent of the federal income tax and legislate that every business with a turnover over one million dollars should spend one percent of its profits on local community projects proportionately in the areas of their workforce, with local people helping to choose the projects. This will make twenty billion dollars available to local communities throughout this nation and demonstrate our trust in the kindness of our fellow citizens.

And our young have lost time for the old. This disconnect leaves the elderly lonely and without purpose, whilst the young miss the benefits of their knowledge and experience. I am going to instigate an educational programme that requires every final-year student to produce a ten-thousand-word account of an elderly stranger's life. The necessary interviews and interaction will create a bond between old and young. It will interrupt loneliness and remind our young students of the debt they owe to those who came before. The experiences of our elderly citizens will inform the future of our youth.

We also need to be kind to our planet and the animals and plants that share it with us. We must combat climate change and allow the planet to restore itself.

This year alone America has suffered almost ten thousand wildfires that have burnt more than twelve million acres of our woodlands. We have sea levels rise by eighteen inches. All our coastal towns are threatened. The Louisiana seaboard, Washington State and Southern Florida are all battling to complete flood defences before they are overwhelmed by sea water. The West Coast has been engulfed by fires, battered again by floods and hurricanes. Fifteen millions of our fellow citizens live under the constant threat of the changing climate. Desertification and soil erosion are increasing rapidly in the southern states, Texas, Arizona and New Mexico. We have abandoned the hydroelectric power stations at Lake Mead and Lake Powell as the river flows have dried up and the Hoover Dam and the Glen Canyon Dam have almost dried up too. Only the diminishing supplies of groundwater, improved methods of water re-cycling and the huge new desalination plants are providing the water we need. We must reverse climate change if America is to survive as a great power for good.

And, fellow Americans, I ask you to study a map of the world. As global warming destroys our vast farmlands of the mid-west through drought and soil erosion it will release land to the north, once inhospitable through cold and ice, but now recovering to release vast mineral wealth and many, many acres of productive farmland. 25% of the northern hemisphere is currently covered by permafrost. Much of this land to be released as farmland is controlled by Russia and it is an unstable Russia that we will rely on for our grain. The Baltic Sea freeze is now a thing of the past and sea trade routes have changed to bring prosperity to Northern Europe. We must reverse climate change if America is to survive as a great power for good.

We have tried carbon capture. We have tried sunshine reflection. We have tried fossil fuel reductions but still the world temperatures continue to rise. Now it is time to let the planet heal itself, to let nature take its course. We must stop the human interventions that have caused this catastrophe for the planet, floods, deserts, soil erosion, loss of wild life habitat and pollution. It's time to be kind to our planet by leaving it alone. It is time to bring an end to animal farming. A plant-based diet would release 70% of our farmland to re-wilding projects. We raise, feed and slaughter 25 million land animals each day here in America. We cut down forests to grow the food they eat and their effluent contaminates our land, our rivers and our seas. 65% of our rivers are classified as being in a poor condition and getting worse. Without animal agriculture we would dramatically reduce methane emissions, use our cropland to feed humans and release 650 million acres of pastureland for re-wilding. We can let the planet restore itself, creating a new carbon sink that will absorb greenhouse gasses and return our planet to the more stable conditions of the 20th century.

I am going to bring forward legislation to make all meals served in public buildings including hospitals, schools and universities to be solely plant based. We will adjust our eating culture to a new normal and if we can't do it we must make sure that our children do.

If we knew how our farm animals are bred and slaughtered, we would choose from the many plant based alternatives. The crowded conditions torture the animals and increase the risk of more pandemics. The devastating MERS43 cost over two million deaths in the US only two years ago. If we all understood the conditions of animal agriculture we would not eat meat from the slaughterhouse or drink milk from the dairy. I will make it obligatory to all food production facilities to be open to public inspection, on request, at least one day each month. More than that, I will pass legislation to ensure that all food producers, from farm to fork, spend two percent of their sales revenue on educational advertising showing exactly how the food is produced. I am providing four billion dollars for a new national enforcement and inspection department and much of the cost will be recovered by the penalties for any inaccurate promotions.

Last year your government spent forty-three billion dollars subsidising the meat and dairy industries. That is almost one hundred and fifty dollars for every man, woman and child in our country. We will phase out the subsidy over the next four years and return the money to you, our taxpayers. A kind America will make kind choices. Kindness will be its own reward, but a reward shared by farm animals and shared by the planet.

And now to public health issues. For too long our medical teams have profited from cures, not prevention. I asked the House E & C Committee to report to me on health prevention methods and to instigate a new educational program. Immediately I am going to bring forward legislation to put health warnings on food products known to be dangerous for the nation's health. This will include high sugar content manufactured foods and all meat and dairy products.

And I will let kindness inform our foreign policy. We will seek understanding not conflict, compromise not friction, accord not quarrel. We have always supported our friends but now we will support our enemies too. The people of this planet all want freedom, peace, shelter and food. We all need to put our differences aside as we strive together to prevent the devastation that is only a generation away if we don't act now. The terrible tragedy of Jakarta, Indonesia, the lost towns on the island of Kiribati, the disappearing resorts of the Maldives, the constant flooding in Pakistan and many threatened coastal towns and cities are only a taste of what is to come. The United States are not immune to disasters from rising sea levels and extreme weather events. We must act now and we must act decisively

This is the radical program our citizens demand and the radical program this country needs for survival. We will be an example for the world to see what kindness delivers. Our actions will be a tribute to our founding fathers without whom we would not be this great nation. God bless America."

Jackson Hendrix James could not implement all these plans in his first term. He was a good man with the best of intentions and his demand for kindness travelled the world.

PART TWO

Hope

In the beginning, how the heavens and the heart

Rose out of chaos.....while it pursues

Things unattempted yet

Paradise Lost

John Milton 1667 (Abridged)

Chapter 25

I have become used to talking to Peter and the predictable machine at least stays quiet when I'm talking. He doesn't gossip, because he has no friends, so I can be frank in front of him. He remembers everything and knows me very well. He knows of my admiration for celebrities.

Knowing an American President was something of a highlight for me, although I never met Hendrix's wife, who was now constantly at his side. There was more to come. I had some interesting experiences as I travelled with Caitlin when she was sent back to Europe as a type of hotel inspector. She had to visit and report on hotels in London, Barcelona, and Moscow. She spent most of her time wondering about her achievement rating at the concurrent inspection of the New Willard in Washington.

I packed carefully for the trip. With almost no daily living expenses and some successful share dealing, I had accumulated a healthy bank account and had always enjoyed an extensive luxury wardrobe purchased in Maine Avenue and City Centre DC, where the luxury brands have their flagship stores. My job demanded a well-presented appearance and clothes were tax allowable. Most shopping was online with same-day delivery by drone, but I liked to browse in stores where eager assistants made me feel important as I ignored the price and selected my clothes. Suits by Luca Faloni and Zegna wrestled with shirts by

Hermes and sweaters by Ralf Lauren in my wardrobe. I now know how wasteful it was.

I accompanied Caitlin for the visits and we started at the Mandarin Hotel in London, then part of the Jin Jiang chain. Caitlin's mission was part of a "spy on your colleagues" program introduced by her Chinese masters after their purchase of the group of hotels. Although China was taking a more liberal attitude to same-sex relationships under the democratic government, the conservative members of the Board of Directors would not have approved of Caitlin's partnership with Aurora.

Caitlin brought me back to Europe for a tour of three sister hotels on which she would be reporting. We had to share a suite, but I had insisted on separate beds. I was still in love with Caitlin, and the idea of sleeping close to her was too difficult to imagine.

Caitlin was still a beautiful, elegant woman with an appealing stillness about her that belied her energy and achievements. She didn't display any vulnerabilities and had a confidence that others might have interpreted as haughtiness. I watched her tall slender frame as she glided around the bedroom naked, body confident and without inhibition. I remembered greedily the first few weeks of our marriage we had of lovemaking, knowing that my lust would now never be returned. Every night for the month of our travels, we were to share a bedroom. Every night I would wonder if I could try to reignite our marriage. Every night I would fail to try. We acted like brother and sister. Our stay at the Mandarin Hotel was memorable, but not because it was a shared time together or because of the hotel.

Whilst in London, I took the opportunity to catch up with Nova and Mia. I had heard that Nova had closed her modelling agency as all fashion items were now displayed using virtual models. Every fashion retailer was using the technique whereby everyone could store their own full body image and see in advance what they would look like in the clothes they were considering. As a result, there were fewer sales returns, but overall revenues plummeted. Few actual images matched the style portrayed in the promotional images. Although the fashion modelling business was in decline, the Jaguar Land Rover Home Building Division was enjoying a boom, and Mia's prosperity more than made up for Nova's inactivity.

Although birth rates continued to fall, migrants entering the United Kingdom, especially from India, created a continuing demand for new homes. Jaguar Land Rover has enabled the government to build the 300,000 required new homes each year. Jaguar had started to develop their own land sites and their comfortable relationship with Sir George Welsh, Minister for Housing, helped the release of more and more land for houses.

Efficient production kept costs low. The standardisation of design had discouraged an aspirational society, although the Jaguar badge was still much sought after. The pod houses were high-technology homes. Each was fitted with LED UVC disinfection lights that killed all viruses and bacteria, a system that had been installed in all hotel rooms since the MERS43 Pandemic. Heating and lights were controlled on entering by early movement sensors, although the brain simulation controls of today were yet to be anything more than an idea. Parcel and shopping deliveries were by drone to rooftop docking stations.

Food requirements were determined by lists from online fridges. Every housing development had a pool of self-driving small electric vehicles that could be called to the home by Metaphone and controlled by Face Recognition Technology. Complex logarithms worked to match the number of vehicles to usage and only very occasionally did households have to wait.

Nova and Mia were totally committed to these high-tech efficient new houses, but they themselves lived in a beautiful Georgian house in the High Street of Farnham, a town in Surrey. They invited Caitlin and me to dinner at their enchanting home. With formal evening wear the requested dress code, I knew that we could expect an old-fashioned English occasion, with the style unchanged for more than 100 years, and so it was.

Caitlin looked stunning in a simple long red dress in Chiltern stretch satin from the Ralf Lauren Collection. A halter silhouette with a tie at the back cascading over her pale back to a dramatic plunging backline. The stretch-infused satin highlighted Caitlin's slim silhouette and small braless breasts with its fluid drape. I was so proud to stand at her side in my grey tuxedo.

Nova had been responsible for the elegant decoration and furnishing that was in keeping with the heritage of the house, built in the days when the Tudor dynasty was ruling England. The house had been restored and clad in Georgian style at the time of mad King George III, about 300 years earlier, when America was still a colony fighting for independence.

It was a warm summer evening. With our fellow guests we had English sparkling wine, now the only affordable alternative to the scarce French champagne, standing on the spacious terrace, overlooking the Mediterranean-style garden. Birdsong in this unusually large garden was soon drowned out by the chatter of the company.

As dusk fell, we left the warm velvet night and entered the cool but cosy dining room where Nova and Mia had organised a dinner party table for the ten of us. All the guests knew that Caitlin and I had been living in Washington and they were curious about the radical ideas of the new charismatic President of the United States. As Caitlin boasted about the number of times the President had stayed with us at The New Willard Hotel, I inwardly smiled, enjoying thoughts about my friendship and discussions with the President but saying nothing. Everybody agreed that it was time the US managed gun control and applauded the

President's policy on animal farming. The thought of a kind America drew some laughter, but I believed that Hendrix would make change possible.

Around the table we discussed change. In England, farming was becoming kinder. The idea of milking cows was already rejected. Probiotic milk had provided a much cheaper and matching alternative, and plant-based milks were forever growing in popularity. Specialist cheese makers kept their own pasture-fed herds, but mass producers used probiotic milk. Jessica, my one-night stand in Australia, must be a very wealthy woman by now.

Laboratory-grown meats were being used to some extent in fast food chains but most of Middle England followed a plant-based diet with only occasional meat or poultry. Sea-caught fish were extremely expensive because of the short supply and the increasing sea pollution. Publicity about the propensity for disease in fish farms and the toxic chemicals used to control it had stifled demand for farmed fish.

Changes in the sea currents in the Atlantic Ocean were still a slumbering threat, but the possibility of changes that would cause unplanned, but devastating climate change was always on the after-dinner agenda amongst the chattering classes. The impacts of the Gulf Stream and the North Atlantic Drift were weakening and the consequences were still unpredictable.

Mia had prepared the dinner and it was delicious. We started with a simple starter of beetroot sweet potato tortellini. Mia had prepared her signature main course, a market thali, kiri hood, tamarind lam, coconut cashew basmati, Gujarati, hari mirch cauliflower, pineapple achar, and flatbread. It was delicious. The balanced flavours and spices left the gentle glow of satisfaction that, together with the plentiful wine, was the perfect encouragement to the easy conversation that flowed across the elegant table.

I was delighted to be sitting between Mia and a local doctor, Adam, who talked confidently about the needs of the National Health Service, suggesting that I visit him for a well-man check-up that I declined. Adam's wife, Jenny, I think, clearly knew that Adam could be a bore when invited to talk about the NHS, but I felt some sympathy for him as I noticed her downturned lips and only half-hidden scowl of general disapproval.

Adam had seen a marked improvement in the health of his patients since the introduction of the Euthanasia Law, three years ago and wondered if it was just because people were frightened to demonstrate illness. The screening program for breast and prostate cancers and improved treatment had almost eliminated death from these diseases, but it was still a challenge to ensure that screening was universal.

Obesity was a continuing problem but in decline because of dietary change and successful drug intervention. Adam's practice concentrated on prevention through diet and exercise. More doctors' surgeries were being in sports clubs.

Adam himself had his practice in the recently refurbished David Lloyd centre in Farnham. He was glad that he didn't have to make the health checks that determined biological age and ended unhealthy lives, now that the tests were all computerised. I didn't admit my unintentional role in the assisted dying policy. I didn't think that one day my life span would be decided by a computer.

Nationally, demand for the health service had fallen dramatically. The general move towards a plant-based diet has started to reduce obesity and the many associated medical conditions. Although plant-based processed meat substitutes have failed to achieve the expected market and the general population has rejected the laboratory-grown meat or the insect protein, many recipes for vegetables have captured the imagination of cooks everywhere in the UK.

The feared resistance to antibiotics had been averted, at least for now, by the latest variation of the drug. The decline in animal farming caused a big reduction in their use. The change from petrol and diesel fuel cars to electric engine vehicles and reduction in travel had improved air quality and Adam had seen a fall in respiratory disease. AI had enabled substantial efficiencies in the use of facilities and waste reduction and the cost of the NHS was at last falling.

Mia was, of course, up and down serving the four-course dinner. Aware that nobody ever asked questions of me and in Mia's absence in the kitchen, I tried to speak to Paul, a gentle man with a quiet voice who sat opposite me across the table. He was quietly engrossed in conversation with Caitlin. I turned to speak with Lucy Crawford, sitting on Mia's right. Lucy was recently widowed when her husband, the Conservative grandee and ex-Minister of State, George Crawford, had become a victim or beneficiary of his own government's policy of assisted dying. He had enjoyed inhabiting the space between reality and imagination that we call politics for over thirty years.

The insincerity of his professional life had impacted his tragic condition. Lucy and George had been married for nearly forty years and she missed him immensely. Despite her loss, she believed that euthanasia was a kind outcome for the 81-years-old politician who suffered from incurable dementia. Lucy was French and I tried talking in my basic schoolboy French, only to find that she had mostly forgotten her mother tongue after so long in the UK. She had lots of gossip about the current government and became less discreet and more vitriolic as the evening progressed. Maybe she just liked me or was pleased to find an audience as she was living alone. Maybe she wasn't used to the wine we all drank.

Lucy believed that the current Prime Minister, Justin Macmillan, looked the part, but had no talent and fewer ideas. He had managed his first term because the labour government had left a growing economy despite their mismanagement. The growth in home ownership, enabled by Nova and Jaguar Land Rover, had improved his natural voter base, especially in the north of England where the high-tech pod houses were most popular.

The NHS waiting lists had disappeared as demand declined and the number of trained doctors had increased following changes made to university places 20 years earlier.

Although numbers had stabilised since the early part of the century the Government still employed half a million Civil Servants. Justin Macmillan had secured a second term by the introduction of a four days working week for Civil Servants, which was only the recognition of current practices throughout industry and commerce.

I suggested that if Justin Macmillan wanted a vanity project to mark his current term in office, he should introduce a grand city tree planting scheme. Proposals since the beginning of the century had stumbled on the horns of austerity, but now the economy was strong, a properly funded proposal could demonstrate the governments' green credentials and provide shade in our warming cities. "Do it big or not it all" was Lucy's contribution but I think that it is no co-incidence that this became the government's flagship announcement at the Party Conference three months later.

As was common in England, cannabis treats were offered with our coffee but only Caitlin, Nova, and Jenny shared them. Relaxed from the treats, Jenny became a different person, full of giggles and very interested in Caitlin, who I could see was flattered by the attention.

As we left the table to spend the late evening in front of the drawing room fire, the tall, slim, well-dressed lady who had sat quietly, opposite me at Jenny's right, married I think to Paul, stopped me at the doorway and told me that we had been to school together. I didn't recognise Emily, Josh's older sister, and provider of my first rejection, almost 30 years ago. She had always been a pretty girl but now she had become stunning. Still very self-assured, strangely, she seemed interested in me. I could see what I took to be a lust-filled glint in her eye as she inspected my body. I immediately invited her for lunch in London the next day, to catch up on old times.

Caitlin was busy with her hotel inspection and was pleased to hear that I was lunching with an old friend. I didn't tell her that it was a woman, or indeed that it was a woman who had been my schoolboy crush, and I had only met again last night. I took the fifteen minutes walk, passing through Hyde Park, from the Mandarin Hotel to the Dorchester Hotel where Emily and I met for lunch. It was another warm and sunny day and the park was full of lunchtime sunbathers. I was happily aware of the many slim tanned bodies on display in the park. I was first to arrive and was quickly taken to our table where I sipped a cold glass of Sauvignon Blanc whilst I waited for my tryst to begin. In pleasant sunshine I was feeling extremely happy. I was in London. When Emily did appear, only a few minutes late, her appearance took my breath away.

My date wore her highest heels, her most elegant long silk-style trousers, and a cotton T-shirt, stretched over her full breasts and deliberately failing to disguise her bra-less nipples. As she walked through the restaurant to the table where I was seated, I noticed every eye in the room embraces her body. I felt a swelling with pride when she arrived at my table and waited for the restaurant manager to arrange her chair. She carried a small overnight bag and, when I enquired as to its purpose, Emily told me that she thought I might want to do something naughty in the afternoon. I was speechless.

Over a leisurely lunch, Emily talked mostly about her own successful career in banking. Her bank was helping finance Mia's housing developments. Her bonuses paid for her big house in Maidenhead. Her stay-at-home husband, Paul, looked after their two teenage children but did nothing to stimulate her with his dull conversation and unexciting love making. I listened attentively and watched her sparkling eyes. She didn't remember our meeting in the bedroom after that gig all those years ago. When I told her what an impression it had been on me, she promised to make it up to me. With lunch enjoyed and an excited tension between us, we went to the room Emily had booked.

Emily seemed to exude a calm stillness in expectation of what was ahead. I was like a puppy on heat in anticipation. Inside the opulent rooms, I tried to kiss Emily but, in a move reminiscent of our earlier encounter, she abruptly stopped me and said that first she must change, glancing meaningfully at her mysterious suitcase. I put the "Do not Disturb" sign on the bedroom door, pulled off my Jacob Cohen blue jeans bought that morning in Harrods, and waited on the bed as Emily went into the bathroom. I lay there uncertain of what to expect and a little frightened.

Was this too good to be true experience some kind of set up? Was I so desperate for love that I was happy to confuse it with sex or so desperate for sex that I could pretend it was love? Was sex without romance worth the effort? Was I being used again or just satisfying my normal male lust? My contemplation was quickly forgotten when Emily reappeared. Perhaps now I would get my own back on the candles.

Emily glided in from the bathroom wearing a sheer mesh button-fronted long-sleeved shirt that whispered tantalisingly over her otherwise naked body. In high-heeled shoes and with the sheer blouse emphasising her full figure, she walked towards the bed. I lay naked on the pure white sheets, willing my manhood to respond, but to no avail. Emily gently stroked my dysfunctional member with no result. She leaned over me, her breasts caressing my chest as she ran her fingers down to my feet and then up my thighs. She nuzzled my stomach, teasing my senses with her tongue. I could not respond and felt more embarrassment. Emily stopped stroking, ran her figures through my tousled hair, whispered that it was okay, and returned to the bathroom.

I quickly dressed. I tugged on my new jeans regretting the

tight sizing that had fuelled my ego only earlier in the day and escaped from the bedroom before she returned and, for the second time, I ran away from Emily, full of embarrassment. Again, the birthday candles had worked their maliferous magic.

Chapter 26

That story made Peter blush! For me, it's just another opportunity lost, another failure in the long list. I never really knew Emily, never had a meaningful conversation, and yet we were ready to share an act of total physical intimacy. Is sex a game society thrusts on us, an expectation to drive our egos? Is it sharing or exploitation? When an organism can be self-induced shouldn't sex be about mental as well as physical closeness, about love, about giving not taking? As my story unfolds you will learn that I am no expert so onwards with my memories.

After only four days in London, Caitlin and I travelled to Barcelona for Caitlin to provide her report on the Mandarin Oriental Hotel in Barcelona. The summer temperatures were unbearable and, although the hotel was busy with brave tourists, the local population was all spending the summer in the north. The boom for holiday homes in Sweden and Norway was a reversal of the trends from the early part of the century. Spain was impoverished by the large number of empty holiday homes.

The climate extremes suffered in the Mediterranean had transformed the region to one of suffocating heat, raging wildfires, and shrinking river flows. Sea levels were rising in spite of the high levels of evaporation that were making the Mediterranean the saltiest sea on the planet. Decreasing oxygen concentrations were killing the sea creatures and destroying the beaches.

The loss of phytoplankton had enhanced the blue of the sea that masked its barren paralysis. Only a few fish survived in the polluted waters. The sea fishing industry was almost destroyed. The growing aquaculture business has failed to compete either as to quantity, price, or taste. The wrecked remains of fish farms were scattered along the Mediterranean coastline like unruly blemishes on a painter's palette, damaged by regulations restricting needed insecticides, hampered by hoards of fish lice, and finally destroyed by rising sea levels and their own toxic chemicals that had polluted the seas. Only fifty years ago ocean caught fish were fed to herbivore cows to encourage milk production. Now a fish meal was a scare and precious commodity.

Circumstances have forced a breakthrough in plant-based eating. Many traditional restaurants were providing plant-based food because of the high cost of fish and meat. Food choices were changing, forced by circumstance despite the previously long-established customer preferences.

Reduction in fossil fuels and the electrification of urban transport had eliminated the Barcelona's air pollution. It was under blue skies of a warm, but not yet hot, early morning when I visited Parc Guell, Gaudi's masterpiece.

I had, of course, visited it many times by virtual experience but nothing prepares you for encountering reality. I couldn't help but contemplate how much we had lost as virtual adventures had destroyed the need for actual experiences. I spent two hours in the garden.

Lost in wonder at the complex mind of Antoni Gaudi and his patron Count Eusebi Guell who had, between them, created this magical and preposterous form of extreme Art Nouveau. The sprawling gardens are larger than I imagined. The columns and forms have lines and curves that mimic nature in vibrant unexpected colour but appeared to me lifelike, harmonious with nature, but from another world. It had attracted mass public attention for over a hundred years. With modern pressures on land scarcity and with a worldwide population of nine billion people to house, it seemed that we no longer had time for the eccentric, the amusing, or the just plain daft. Gaudi's work is a reminder to all future generations that there is more to life than just living.

Soon it was too hot to remain outside and, as the park cleared, I returned to the hotel in a whimsical mood.

After a short swim in the hotel pool, I showered, and slipped into my Valentino white cotton shirt, Tom Ford chinos, and Stella McCartney sneakers to meet Caitlin for lunch. She introduced me to Bartoli Sanchez, the Spanish Minister for Agriculture, who was staying at the Mandarin Oriental and would join us for lunch.

Bartoli Sanchez was a portly man with a red face, a large

moustache, and the appearance of a life threatened by his enjoyment of it. However, he turned out to be much less fun in our company than his appearance suggested. We lunched at the Moments Restaurant where Raul Balam was maintaining his mother's reputation for creative fresh and healthy cuisine inspired by Catalan culinary culture, but now almost entirely plant-based. Our meal was fantastic and the service and taste fully deserve the Michelin three-star reputation.

Bartoli expressed his concern that the ingredients for a traditional Spanish diet were no longer available in the markets. Spanish cooks were having to learn new skills, but he felt that he was providing more variety for both consumers and suppliers.

Almost twenty-five percent of the Spanish aquifers had dried up and water availability had decreased by about ten percent. Pests and disease had increased in the warmer temperatures and plant yields generally were seven percent below the levels of earlier in the century.

The grape yields in wine-producing areas were down by twenty percent this year. With constantly rising temperatures, Spain was facing the loss to desertification of the Dehesa, the vast 2.3 million hectares of woodland in the south and west, across large parts of Andalusia and Extremadura.

I asked Bartoli why the Spanish government hadn't

condemned factory farming and animal slaughter like they had in the UK and were planning in America. By promoting a ban, the government would take the initiative on moral and ethical grounds and appear in control rather than at the mercy of events. Caitlin told him how impressed we were by the US President's plans expressed in his Inaugural Speech. It represented hope for the future that we should all share. Bartoli could only anticipate social and economic difficulties for southern Europe. He believed that there was no chance of reversing the climate disaster that had brought the insufferable summer temperatures whilst worldwide greenhouse gas emissions continued to increase.

I'd entered the restaurant celebrating the beauty of the natural world, the complex vision of Gaudi, and the elegance of our surroundings, only to be hauled into the reality of a country in crisis.

I tried to change the subject to our proposed afternoon visit to the football museum at the Camp Nou Stadium. This historical landmark, protected by planning regulations, was now unused and unloved but housed a memorable football museum that Aurora had recommended to Caitlin. I wondered why our guest didn't want to discuss it, but later I would find out.

Bartoli became uneasy as the restaurant filled. If the press caught him eating in such sumptuous surroundings, he would suffer social media condemnation for months and probably never recover his political credibility. Many of our fellow guests would be wearing the concealed body cameras that had become popular as a form of protection from wrong accusations and, although it was unlikely amongst the wealthy society that frequented the Moments Restaurant, these cameras could be directed at our table and leaked on social media. Bartoli said his polite goodbyes, leaving Caitlin and me in a somber mood that we hoped our visit to Nou Camp would reverse.

The visit to the football museum was a disaster. Neither Caitlin nor I were football fans, and we had only been persuaded to make this visit by Aurora's late-night telephone call to Caitlin. The once famous Nou Camp was a skeleton of a building, a ghost town of football memories now that the Barcelona men were playing in the indoor Conchi Amancio Stadium in the Peguera district.

Support for the growing success of the Barcelona Women's team had been enhanced by the declining fanbase of the men's team. The introduction of cheerleaders, in-game pop music, statistics flashed on giant screens and a rigorous interpretation of the rules had changed football from the tribal man's sport of the early part of the century to a family occasion. The quantity of popcorn was as important as the number of goals. The more family-friendly women's football had attracted much greater sponsorship and flourished leaving the men playing catch up.

A new one hundred thousand seat Conchi Amancio stadium had been built as part of the regeneration of Peguera in the north of the city and named after Spain's first lady football superstar. We didn't visit the roofed stadium or see the simplicity of the design with family boxes rather than rows of seats and air conditioning to regulate the temperature but wished we had experienced the more vibrant community. The day wasn't going well and for me, it did not improve.

Bored Caitlin suggested visiting the rooftop Sky Bar in the Axel Hotel and I found myself in Barcelona's coolest gay bar, recently renovated in 1920s style with red velvet sofas and flowers everywhere. I felt uncomfortable with so many friendly, beautiful, part-naked bodies on show. I felt embarrassed that my birth gender still mattered to me. The people in the bar were kind, gentle, and inclusive and I started to question my own sexual orientation.

After all, Caitlin was my wife and best friend but not my lover. Faced with the alluring and provocative Emily, I had failed to achieve any arousal. Life as a pretend husband and acting big brother to Caitlin did provide security and company, but I also needed some proper romance. Perhaps I would find it with another man.

I had one glass of rather ordinary champagne and, feeling in her shadow, I left when Caitlin started a deep conversation with a rather busty blonde who was wearing a man's jacket and billowing silk trousers over her otherwise naked torso. I took a convey car back to my hotel, my hot feet sore in my new sneakers and with the idea of a gay relationship banished from my sober thoughts. When Caitlin didn't return until the next morning, I wondered what Aurora would think if she knew how her suggested outing had ended.

We were still in Barcelona when the Goodstone scandal hit the headlines throughout the world. Olivia Goodstone, thirty-two, worldwide superstar, captain and scorer of two goals in England's 2035 World Cup win, model, social media personality of the year for six consecutive years, owner of the UK's largest group of Start-Up Football Academies and Secretary of State for Sport in the Tory government, had been charged with six counts of having sexual activity with a child under 13 and possession of prohibited images.

The press speculated that the huge chain of Start-Up Football Academies was just a cover for female predators to attract young girls to share sexual experiences. There was a witch hunt to expose anyone who had been aware of her activities and had not spoken out. I was just relieved that she had not visited the Sandringham Hotel again whilst Caitlin was manager.

I was thankful that Sandringham wasn't caught up in a press enquiry that, in the end, exposed eight members of her academy staff who shared Goodstone's unacceptable wrongdoings. I wondered if Josh would be relieved that they had not met despite my best efforts. The scandal would rock the Justin Macmillan government. Their response was some crowd-pleasing legislation that would have a popular outcome.

Chapter 27

I don't like to wander off subject, but this was a time in my life when the remembered experiences camouflaged the boredom of hotel rooms, disagreements with Caitlin, and my lack of purpose as I travelled in her wake. My purpose now is just to tell my story before I die. I must tell you about our final hotel inspection, our visit to Moscow, and how I met Anastas. Caitlin and I went to Russia to inspect the Mandarin Oriental Hotel. It wasn't a great visit, but I did meet Anastas, who would one day be such a help to me.

After Barcelona, Moscow was a shock. The Mandarin Oriental Hotel has river frontage opposite the Kremlin. First planned to open in 2021, delayed by the COVID pandemic, and then by the Western embargo on trade with Russia after the invasion of Ukraine, the hotel had not opened until 2036. Only ten years later, it was looking tired.

I was shocked to see so many identical petrol motor vehicles noisily running on the streets of Moscow and to smell the toxic exhaust fumes. These cars were not yet driverless, and the streets were full of road signs and with stop lights at junctions. The vehicles even used separate direction lanes on the roads for each way of travel. I had become accustomed to the quieter cities of Western Europe where city travel was almost exclusively in driverless electric conveycars that were monitored by satellite with no fear of collision. Throughout Western Europe, the control of personal vehicles by satellite has eliminated the need for road signs or single-way traffic.

With the selfish arrogance of earlier governments, the Social Democracy Party of Pavel Pasternak had not introduced electric cars, installed electric charging points, or charged roads. The nation was continuing with petrol and diesel cars to utilise the vast reserves of Russian oil. Global warming did not seem a problem for this northern country without care for the future of the planet. Without an international market for their petrol vehicles, the only Russian motor manufacturer that had survived was AvtoVAZ and their Lada cars were everywhere. They were not too reliable, and Muscovites still joked that the last six pages of the Lada user manual were the bus and train timetables.

The death of Putin, almost 20 years ago, had enabled the eventual return to normal international trading. Demand for Russian oil and gas had almost totally collapsed as countries developed sustainable energy security. Suspicion and uncertainty had frustrated many trading arrangements and only now was business returning to the levels of the beginning of the century.

The years of political and economic isolation had damaged Russian prosperity, but the melting of the coastal sea ice had opened up trade with both Shanghai and Rotterdam. Russia was to become the trading centre we recognise today. With global warming potentially releasing thousands of hectares of frozen land in Siberia and the migration of South Asian refugees providing cheap labour, it was expected that Siberia would become the breadbasket of the world. The permafrost in 13 million square kilometres of the tundra was starting to melt releasing carbon into the atmosphere, amplifying the climate change, but opening huge areas of Russia for farming and grain production. Many new swamps and lakes needed engineered solutions The farming production possibilities were easy to see.

The hotel was busy with consultants and lobbyists from all over the world, competing for a share of the expected business. Migration from Asia was fuelling a demand for housing, schools, and hospitals as workers were needed to exploit the opportunities created by the newly planned agriculture and mineral recovery industries. Siberia was the new frontier for business and every major international company was anxious not to miss out. The Kremlin Government was the first obstacle to overcome, and Moscow was the only place to do it.

The manager of The Mandarin Oriental, Maxim Devin, introduced us to his son. Anastas was then 24 years old, tall and dark with a sculptured body that made him look elegant in his tailored suit. He spoke perfect English. He had just completed his study of politics in America at Harvard University, where he had been a big fan of fellow alumnus, now President Jackson Hendrix James. When I told him that I had met President James at the New Willard he was fascinated to hear more. I had little to tell other than that the

President was a kind, polite, and humble man who could be a role model for us all.

Anastas and I found easy conversation and laughed together about the ridiculous silly things we noticed whilst Caitlin and Maxim talked about the hotel business. Most elderly businessmen seemed to employ very young pretty personal assistants. We both felt that they must be very personal as few demonstrated any business skills. There was also a big growth in powerful women executives visiting the hotel. Whilst short men preferred tall young lady personal assistants it was different for the many female executives. It seemed that power in women was still dependent upon their towering height. When the lady executives were accompanied by male personal assistants, they seemed to select a short man to emphasise the height of the female superior. Anastas could always recognise computer dating companions in bars and restaurants. He had lots of tales of mismatches and hurried departures.

When Anastas suggested that he show me around Moscow the next day, whilst Caitlin was at work, I jumped at the opportunity. We had a great day. Starting at the hotel we walked on the banks of the Moskva River to the cobblestones of Red Square where I was overwhelmed by the size of the Kremlin. This magnificent two hundred and seventy thousand square meters complex is the imposing site of the President's home and offices, cathedrals, and a museum, all surrounded by walls built in the fifteenth century. We saw the Putin Mausoleum adjacent to, but overshadowing the Lenin Mausoleum. I speculated that both were built in celebration of the fall from power, rather than a commemoration of the achievements of the deceased inhabitants. They remain a tool of the propaganda that elevates politicians above their citizens.

We marvelled at the fairytale Byzantine and Asian design of St Basil's Cathedral, built in 1555 but still one of the most photographed buildings in the world in 2046. From the Red square, we walked for fifteen minutes to the Bolshoi Theatre, where the most famous ballet company regularly performs, and admired its Neoclassical splendour. We took the famous subway the twenty minutes' journey to Gorky Park and strolled between the flower beds as Anastas told me his ambition. He was about to start as a trainee hotel manager for a rival hotel chain, a job organised by his father. He really wanted to enter politics.

The military command that had assumed control after the death of Putin and continued the authoritarian government had stepped aside in 2038 and arranged a Presidential election.

With opposition groups still splintered and unable to promote a coherent shared policy, the United Russia Party had swept back into power with a policy of territorial expansion and imperial ambitions. The young soldiers' deaths and the economic depravations of the lost war in Ukraine had been forgotten and Vladimir Putin's political party was back in government. They had now held power for two terms. An election was looming and Anastas was supporting the Liberal Democratic Party, a modernising opposition.

Anastas had an enthusiasm for his cause that I had not seen since Bess all those years ago. A less authoritarian government would unleash the initiative and competitive nature of the Russian population and better relationships with Western markets to enable the exploitation of the immense natural reserves and the improving strategic position of the country.

Not wanting to upset Maxim, I advised Anastas to follow his father's advice and enter the hospitality industry. The opportunities to travel would enrich his world understanding and most importantly the hotel business would teach him how to listen. It would educate him in the skills of persuasion and remind him that it's not what you say that counts, it's what your audience hears. I told him of the importance of kindness and how greed, whether territorial or financial, was so destructive of a fruitful life.

Friendship, between individuals and nations, was a universal expectation only thwarted by power-mad national leaders. Anastas agreed and pledged that we would be friends forever. We met again many years later when Anastas had fulfilled some of his ambitions. I am proud to have spent that day with a charismatic young friend finding his way in life and that he remembered our time together when I needed his help.

Chapter 28

I liked Europe. I liked travel and still had the energy of youth, but I was relieved to be getting back to America. Every country has its own smell, and the US still had the smell of optimism. Maybe if I had stayed there, I wouldn't now be facing the end of my life and be rushing to tell my story. New York holds some good memories because it was here where I met Georgina for the first time, although I didn't know then what an impact she would have on my life.

We were returning to the New Willard Hotel in Washington with a short stopover in New York. Even in the airport reception hall, the mood of America had changed. The atmosphere was calm and welcoming. None of the airport staff, border control, or regular police were wearing guns. The specialist anti-terror forces were clearly identified by their red helmets and automatic rifles. By Presidential decree, all public servants were required to leave their guns at home. The full legislation on gun control had still to be agreed in the face of intense lobbying by the NRA and resistance from the cowboy states of Texas, Colorado, Utah, and Kansas. Gun crime had diminished in the city centres as gun carrying was seen as cowardly and unnecessary when law enforcement could not respond in kind and the death penalty for disregarding the law was so unambiguous.

After the noise of Moscow, the thousands of silent conveycars that raced around New York streets, somehow always managing to avoid each other, were amazing. With road traffic controls not required, the apparent confusion was accident-free, but I was glad that all pedestrian walkways were high above street level.

In New York, Caitlin was joined by Aurora and I again moved into an adjoining bedroom. We stayed at the Mandarin Oriental on the Upper West Side. The three of us went to an intimate, nostalgic Ariana Grande performance at the Chelsea Music Hall under Chelsea Market. Caitlin and Aurora had been big fans of Ariana Grande since 2011 when Ariana was only 18 years old, but they told me that she had not lost her magic 35 years later as they sang along with her tunes from yesteryear.

At the concert, I was less impressed by her music than her altruism. Ariana Grande has always been a vocal supporter of human right especially the right of transgender visibility. Once an individual's right to decide their sexual identity had been widely acknowledged, Ariana had devoted much of her time and immense wealth to the cause of animal rights.

On this evening of music, the guest appearances from a tired-looking Miley Cyrus and a still attractive Billie Eilish were used to express their activism for animals. Billie Eilish was amazing with the simple clarity of her voice not influenced by the increasing visibility of her Tourette's syndrome. All three performers spoke of the right of every sentient being to have a natural life. An animal's life is as important to that animal as our life is to us. They condemned the exploitation of all animals but left their greatest vitriol for animal farming. The mass slaughter of farm animals for human food was still a modern-day holocaust and although many citizens in the US had turned to a plant-based diet there was still much to do. They all received loud cheers from an audience that was beginning to share the kindness demanded by their President.

We returned to the hotel and had a nightcap in the bar. When Caitlin and Aurora retired to their room, I stayed pondering my teenage years when the songs of Ariana Grande and Billie Eilish were the soundtrack of my life when I had an optimism for achievements that I had never reached. I reminded myself that I was still attractive, well-mannered, and experienced. I wondered how I had so failed to find a partner to love and to love me.

As though she was reading my thoughts, a good-looking lady at the bar asked if she could join me for a last drink. She introduced herself as Georgina, a British national on business in New York. I was happy for the diversion before I became melancholy. I was tired and a little squiffy from the drinks and nearly refused but I was jealous of Caitlin and Aurora and lonely at the thought of a night alone in my bedroom after two weeks of sharing with Caitlin on our travels. I sat and talked to Georgina, wondering whether I should invite her to my skyline suite on the 53rd floor overlooking Central Park, for a final nightcap and more. Fearing rejection or erectile dysfunction, I did not have the courage for the invitation that I felt sure would have been accepted.

From the bar, the lights of New York were an inspiring sight, a tribute to the achievement and consumption of the human will, and brave architecture in a collapsing world. Bored by drinking champagne in crystal glasses, I ordered a vegan hot chocolate, and Georgina had one too. I wasn't listening to her idle small talk as I admired the amazing terrace window with its panoramic view of New York and the built beauty of my surroundings. When I turned and observed Georgina, I realised that she was an exquisite woman, still youthful, with irresistible piercing blue eyes, clear skin, a freckled round face and button nose. Her whole face lit up when she smiled, and her smile was never far away. I felt unbelievably sad. With a warming hot chocolate in my hand, I sat comfortably on the elegant sofa and opened my heart like never before. I, who abhorred self-pity and hated casting myself as a victim, talked about myself for at least an hour. I explained the disappointment and disgust I felt. I disclosed how I had traded having a privileged life with Caitlin, for a proper family and somebody to love.

All my frustrations and disappointments translated into tears of loathing. My pointless life was a kaleidoscope of missed opportunities that I described to my lone audience, a total stranger.

Georgina was a kind woman. She listened without interruption as the words flew from my quivering mouth. Only when I stopped, surprised at my outpouring and exhausted by the emotions, did she speak. In a comforting tone, Georgina reminded me that I was still young and that the experiences of my youth gave me the knowledge to do something that would make a difference in society. I had a lot to give if I found the passion to change. I was only a victim if I allowed myself to believe it. I could use the apparent confidence I had pretended, to good effect if I tried. She had suffered years of doubt and worry until she had found her place in life. There was nothing that I couldn't do if I wanted. I was born with every advantage, health, intelligence, a good education, and an open-faced appearance. I slipped my head on her chest. Comforted by the warmth of her body, the assurance of a hug, and sleepy after a busy day I snoozed at her side until she suggested it was bedtime.

My bedroom seemed a lonely place when I finally fell into my bed, alone again.

I felt embarrassed in the morning. I had never shown my vulnerability or exposed my emotions like I had to Georgina. I had not invited Georgina to talk about herself. It would be many years later that I was to hear her story. The next day, in an act of kindness, she suggested that we lunch together. I thought that there must have been a spark between us but now I know it was just Georgina's warm heart and the empathy that she offered to everyone, not just me. Caitlin and I were going back to the New Willard in Washington DC, and I had to refuse lunch. I didn't see Georgina again for three years.

Chapter 29

Telling my story brings me back to life. It's 4:00 pm and darkness is descending. I hope that it will be a warm evening again, but without the tropical storm that interrupted yesterday's final night's sleep. I love to hobble into my garden and listen to the sound of the evening crickets and remember the now-forgotten cheerful chirping of the grasshoppers that used to populate the garden.

At least we still have the hum of bees that circle the lavender beds. I am still hoping for a visitor tonight. I feel some melancholy that Peter is my only companion, and he is a robot, bought and paid to be my company. It was so different at the New Willard Hotel.

Returning to the New Willard in Washington from New York was like returning home after a long holiday. The comfort of familiarity was clouded by the despair of old routines. I was determined to change my life after my sorry encounter with Georgina. I was quite wealthy after my share dealings in Shanghai, but I had done nothing with my life except act as a charming host at Caitlin's side. I had to do something in my own name, but what?

Watching the athletes performing in the one-hundred and fiftieth anniversary of the modern Olympics taking place in Greece only served to emphasise my lack of achievement. I had not followed through on my school time success as a sprinter. I felt jealous of the men who had devoted themselves to excellence whilst I had just chased the easy way.

The hotel was buzzing as always with political gossip, and I moved between the guests, anonymous to them, but collecting information that often was very profitable. My growing share portfolio gave me little pleasure or feeling of self-worth. I remember my despair, hidden by my smiles but very real for me. Restless nights when ideas endlessly repeated themselves were only to be cast aside in the reality of morning. I had to do something useful and make my contribution to society.

Overhearing the climate experts who stayed at the New Willard as they prepared to present their predictions to the White House, I realised the enormity of the problem faced by the world and the apparent lack of popular understanding. The world's population was choosing to ignore the approaching calamity. Even the US could not avert disaster alone. Each country was waiting for leadership and example as every government feared facing the short-term economic and political cost of the necessary climate change legislation.

Politicians were fearful of exposing the frightening truth. It was meat, fish, and dairy consumption and the growing intense animal farming, not fossil fuels, that was exhausting natural resources, polluting the seas, and the main cause of global warming. Big business had too much to lose by being honest. The press was dependent on the meat and dairy industry for advertising. Schools, universities, and even animal charities were sponsored by the polluters responsible for the greenhouse gas emissions and land misuse. The courageous ambition of President Jackson James had made little progress in the last two years.

I was picking up information on climate change as I was listening for commercial information for my share dealing. I had easy access to the best brains in the field as they stayed at the hotel, all too willing to share their knowledge and their fears with me. But if I was going to reach the wider public, I had to find a way to present the information that would help the population to engage. Knowing no better way, I decided to tell my life story. I would call my book *The Future Past of an Extraordinary Man.* I am delighted that you are reading it.

It was the great storm of January 2047 that finally encouraged me to start writing. The torrential rain had coincided with a high tide and high winds. The storm combination and the rise in sea levels caused extensive flooding throughout the city. The New Willard Hotel didn't escape the devastation. Despite recently increased premiums, the insurance companies were overwhelmed by claims from Washington and along the US's east coast.

New Orleans was hit yet again and was becoming a ghost town, a city no longer habitable following a 45cm rise in sea levels and frequent storm surges. The severe weather was circulating the earth and news around the world was of severe flooding. My parents in the UK were alright in their Surrey home but the UK's coastal beaches had all disappeared and some two hundred thousand coastal homes were no longer habitable. In Humberside, Norfolk, and East Anglia large areas of farmland were threatened by rising sea levels. Homes and businesses in London's wealthy areas of Chelsea and Westminster were only protected by the new Thames flood protection barrier constructed at a cost of £20 billion.

The Netherlands sea defences were breached and Amsterdam, two and a half metres below sea level suffered its worst flood for 16 years as a quarter of its buildings were underwater and three hundred thousand people were displaced. All around the world, huge populations experienced the horrors of flooding. In New York, the 9/11 Memorial, Battery Park, and Ellis Island were all underwater. In Mumbai, the Mahalakshmi Temple and the Haji Ali Mosque were flooded. In Tokyo, the airport was submerged. These tragedies had long been predicted and in some instances, they were simply events from which there would be no recovery.

The New Willard closed for renovation after the flooding, giving me the privilege of time. For a month I sat in the first-floor hotel library writing my book. This private story was seldom interrupted by conversation, but I was delighted by the return of hotel guests as visiting climatologists, economists or concerned politicians would talk to me about the dangers of climate change and the solutions that would inform my story. The fact-finding was a depressing time for me.

Endless experts used my easy attention to test their theories, explain their research and allow me to scrutinise their analysis. Nobody offered an alternative prognosis to the inevitability of a manmade warming climate that would cause loss of habitat, water shortage, extreme weather events, famine, and floods leading to mass migration. Our only hope was to end animal farming, re-wild the pastures, restore natural habitat, and let the Earth recover itself. Our selfish, shortsighted population would not accept change on the scale needed, and, eventually, our species would be the last on Earth to become extinct. Having destroyed the habitat of so many wild animals we were now destroying our own.

Scared by the thought I wrote every day, and my book was written in two months and, fortunately, accepted by the first publisher to read it. Promoted by my many celebrity friends and acquaintances it was soon a best seller, and this my life story became public property.

Chapter 30

My study here looks over a public footpath that runs alongside the front of my home. As dog walkers pass I always try to offer a wave of acknowledgement. Over time I have enjoyed the friendliness of the more regular acquaintances. One unnamed friend passes now, in the growing darkness with her headlight flashing through falling leaves. As I watch her gentle stride I wonder if she will miss our irregular contact. What would she think if she knew that by tomorrow, I would not be here ever again? I mustn't start feeling sorry for myself as I have reached a more positive situation in the story of my life.

I went alone to Israel for a brief holiday that coincided, by chance, with the celebration of 100 years since the founding of Israel and the peace talks that produced an unexpected result. In 1947, after the holocaust of the Second World War, the United Nations agreed on a plan to partition Palestine into two states giving British-controlled land to provide a permanent home for the Jewish Nation. This would fulfil a promise made to Jewish people to gain their support in the 1914 - 18 World War. Many hundreds of thousands of Jewish people had resettled from Europe and more followed to the consternation of the Arabs living there.

The brutal exclusion of Arabs living in this part of Palestine and the sale of their land and property to Jewish owners on the establishment of a Jewish state had angered the

Palestinians and they, and the Arab nations, continued to oppose the partition. Military action between the two areas has festered ever since. There seemed to be no solution as the opposing parties in a conflict that flared from time to time left both communities in a state of insecurity.

The unimaginable Israeli retribution on the people of Gaza in 2024 had left a permanent scar. Jerusalem, the Capital city of Israel, had a history of conflict over many generations with wars over the religious shrines important to Judaism, Christianity, and Islam. The Temple Mount is widely considered the holiest place on Earth. Israel considered Jerusalem to be wholly part of Israel since the annexation of East Jerusalem from Jordan in 1980, but the United Nations still did not accept Israeli sovereignty.

The Palestinians, supported by Arab nations, did not accept Israel as a state. With reduced demand for oil and much reduced national incomes, the Arab states did not want a continuing conflict that was hard to finance. Israel, so long dependent on the US for support, was also ready to make concessions for a lasting peace. The charismatic Afan Abdallah was a leader of the Palestinian people and he had made a strong case for his people over the social media channels and to talk show hosts throughout America. Nobody expected the traditionalist Prime Minister of Israel, Caleb Goldman, to accept his proposal.

However, on the one-hundredth anniversary of the establishment of the state of Israel, the state of Palestine recognised Israel as a free state and Israel recognised Palestine as an independent state west of the Jordan River, occupying the West Bank and Gazza Strip. Both states would give equal rights to all citizens whether Muslim, Christian, or Jewish, and Palestinians would have unencumbered access to the religious places in Jerusalem. With the approval of all 193 member states of the United Nations in the General Assembly, peace would be restored at last.

Celebrations in Jerusalem were muted. I was staying at the Waldorf Astoria on Agron Street and a grand ball had been organised to mark the occasion. Alone, and not knowing anybody, I wandered between the couples hoping to find an entry into conversation somewhere. Eventually, I noticed the Israeli author, Abigail Pereira, from the book cover of her discourse Climate Change in the Middle East. Her book recorded that the temperature rises in the Middle East was half a degree every ten years, twice the world average. Ms. Pereira predicted that the consequent water shortage and increased dust storms would threaten agricultural production and human health.

With political instability, Iraq, Iran, Lebanon, Yemen, and Syria had ignored the problem but in other countries, large-scale desalination plants were in the early stages of construction or planning, because of her campaigning. Finding an excuse to talk to this charming, elderly lady, I congratulated her on this achievement, and fortunately, she had read my book and was happy to talk.

Abigail felt that she had not done enough. Average temperatures in the Middle East had risen by three degrees, causing a thirty percent reduction in rainfall, the drying up of groundwater, and greater seawater evaporation. Two hundred and twenty thousand tonnes of naturally occurring hydrocarbon gases rise annually from the Red Sea every year and, mixed with industrial emissions, cause increasing health issues for the ports and resorts of several countries, including Egypt, Jordan, Saudi Arabia, and Israel. The over exploitation of marine resources, illegal disposal of pollutants by vessels, pollution from tourists' hotspots, and urban and industrial waste, were causing habitat destruction. The Dead Sea had already disappeared into sinkholes as the retreating sea left infertile unstable land despite the Israeli, Jordanian, and Palestinian projects to pump brine into it from the desalination plant on the Red Sea. Even the new one hundred- and seventy-kilometres linear city of Neom in Saudi Arabia, built alongside four hundred and fifty kilometres, of the Red Sea for nine million inhabitants, was finding problems in rehousing the residents migrating from the temperatures of Riyadh.

We celebrated the peace treaty but mourned the temperature changes that made living so difficult, storms more damaging, water so scarce, and the disappearing beaches as sea levels rise. The lack of local food production because of damaged agricultural land required imported food delivered by damaging transport on oil-fuelled boats to create a never-ending cycle of destruction and despair. This disastrous cycle was causing further pollution and more unusable agricultural land. Government targets for the better use of water were constantly missed. Desalination plants filtered salt water for human consumption but were insufficient to support agriculture in a meaningful way. There seemed to be no way to resolve the problems faced by the Middle East.

I left Jerusalem realising that warfare was a petty problem compared to the impact of climate change, and I was resolved to use my minor celebrity to spread the understanding to a still unbelieving population.

October 2048 COP54 New York USA

COP54 had continued the tradition of a virtual conference. Temperatures had continued to rise and were now 1.8 degrees above pre-industrial norms. Sea levels have risen 45cm since the beginning of the century. Sea pollution have spread to every ocean. Fish stocks were almost exhausted. Fresh drinking water was becoming a scarce resource for many communities. The world population have reached 9.5 billion. CO2 emissions continued to rise.

Chapter 31

I do feel that, despite my book sales, by the middle of the century I had still made little or no change to the general understanding of the climate change emergency, animal welfare and general health. Any big changes we were seeing came from government intervention. Life on our planet was improving. It certainly improved for me when I escaped the political conversations in Washington because I met Georgina again.

I recognised her tall frame as she walked through the hotel door pushing her travel bag, holding a rather large elaborate hat whilst she arranged her tousled hair. Her freckled face shone with good health without makeup and her ever-ready smile sparkled in her eyes. I had been imagining this moment since New York. I don't think she recognised me until I walked over to reception and, using my status as the husband of the manager, I suggested that Caitlin would like this guest upgraded as she is an old friend.

The look of surprise on Georgina's face turned to understanding as she remembered me from our brief meeting, some three years ago. Her natural smile played on my heart as she asked, "You have still not changed?" Was it a question or a statement that she directed towards me after an initial polite expression of thanks?

I felt alarmed at how beautiful she was and how pathetic I

must seem to her. Only when she said, "We must have that lunch together," did I feel that I must have left some sort of impression and perhaps we could be friends.

Over lunch together the next day I was able to tell Georgina that, although my domestic arrangements had not changed, I was not feeling sorry for myself since having my book on climate change published. I boasted that *The Future Past of an Extraordinary Man* had become a worldwide success, and I was a minor celebrity amongst the climatologist fraternity.

Although I didn't tell Georgina, my wealth from the share dealing since Shanghai and the income from my book had made me a wealthy man. As I was no longer dependent on Caitlin for my way of life I felt quite comfortable living as her husband, rent-free in wonderful hotels. However, sitting comfortably with Georgina was again reminding me of what I was missing.

This time I did encourage Georgina to talk about herself. I learnt that she had been a moderately successful professional tennis player. She married a handsome and successful lawyer when she was only 19. He proved to be abusive. He had never used physical violence but insisted on controlling her movements. Her tennis career was halted, and full-time work was forbidden. Her friendships were discouraged. He demanded practices of sexual dominance to destroy her confidence. He refused to have children. The marriage had lasted seventeen years before Georgina had the courage to walk away from the glamorous lifestyle he provided.

With a good job now secured, Georgina wondered why she had surrendered her own personality to the bullying. At last, she had belief in herself. She had acquired a love of opera during her marriage as she had accompanied her ex-husband when he entertained clients at London's Royal Opera House. She had a ticket to see Carmen at the War Memorial Opera House as she passed through San Francisco, and I wished I could join her. The story of love and betrayal reminded me that love can only be given, not taken. I was ready to give my love, but would Georgina take it?

Georgina was stopping over in Washington DC for sightseeing on her way to Los Angeles, where she was doing a location search for Disney Pictures. The film company was producing a documentary about the search for a Mars landing. She was negotiating the filming of the early headquarters of Space-X in Hawthorne and was to be in San Francisco for two days before driving up to Los Angeles. I made my excuses to Caitlin and booked my plane ticket to San Francisco for a two-night stay at the Four Seasons Hotel.

Georgina was staying at the nearby Ritz Carlton. I spent two days sightseeing in San Francisco with Georgina. We rode the trams, strolled over Baker Beach for the best views of Golden Gate Bridge, ate street food on Fisherman's Wharf, and played 20th-Century arcade slot machines at the Musee Mecanique. We giggled over the service in Shizen and marvelled at the creativity of the menu in Wildseed.

Georgina was funny, relaxed, and easy to be with. I was walking on air, smiling at strangers, and happier than I could remember. And then she was gone.

I called Caitlin from San Francisco that night and announced that I was leaving her.

I rented a cottage in Baker Beach for one month whilst I decided what to do with my life. I couldn't follow Georgina, as I had no idea how she felt about me and, anyway, she was working, but she had given me the courage and confidence to finally make the change I had feared for the last twelve years even though I lacked the bravery to do it face to face.

It was two lonely days later when Georgina texted to say her work was complete and could she see me in Washington on her way back to London. I explained that I had left Caitlin and the hotel and was living in a beachside cottage in San Francisco. I invited her to stay on her route home. I was nervous that she would not want me, couldn't fancy me physically, and that if she did, I would not be able to perform after so many years of abstinence. I prepared both bedrooms with clean sheets, put flowers in the bathrooms, and persuaded myself it would be an overnight sleepover.

Georgina stayed for the rest of the month and we only needed one bedroom. My early impotence soon forgotten in the excitement of the passion I felt for Georgina. Our lovemaking was both intense and gentle and our coupling complete. I knew instantly that I had at last found somebody special to love and be loved by. With Georgina, I knew who I wanted to be. Again, I never thought to ask Georgina whether she shared my dream of an heir.

I returned to England with Georgina and at last, my life was joyful again. Georgina showed me the importance of family and friends and her life demonstrated the futility of material things, the wastefulness of designer clothes and contrived appearance, and the pretentiousness of the rich and spoilt. She treated everybody the same, whether rich or poor, old or young, kind or callous. Georgina was comfortable in her own skin, less disciplined than Caitlin, and less needy. Confident about herself Georgina didn't worry about a few extra pounds or wearing last year's fashion. She always had a project and a passion and care for those without a voice, the abused and uncared for whether human or animal.

For a while, I had forgotten the climate disasters faced by others and the unnecessary suffering of farm animals. Reality returned when I saw what could happen when a caring society changed its diet. The UK demonstrated how far the rest of the world had to travel to meet the challenge, but it could be done.

Chapter 32

The UK was doing well, but much of the world was a long way behind. Most would catch up eventually. I am lucky to live to see the changes, but so soon I will have to leave this planet. Maybe November is as good a time as any to pass away. The hot, dry summer is over and colder nights are upon us.

The inconsistent tropical rainstorms make any travel planning impossible for a few months. I don't like the idea of a lonely Christmas surrounded by anxious well-wishers pretending to care or, even worse, only Peter for company. I have nothing to live for but life itself and that seems very precious now. If only I could live to see another Spring. I find the re-emergence of garden shrubs an annual surprise. Forgotten charms, surprise new birth, and the smell of the world starting again all speak of spring. It was in springtime, May 2050, that there was the first election that I had been around to vote in for a few years.

The election campaign in England was for the first time, dominated by concerns about climate change and the impact of global warming that now seemed inevitable. The lack of preparation for rising sea levels and extreme weather conditions by the Justin Macmillan government came under a lot of criticism. The connection to Olivia Goodstone and the continuing public enquiry about her organised sex offending was routinely raised by his young Labour opponent Henry Williams.

The Labour leader was only thirty-eight years old and had a glittering business career in banking and was now a well-used media pundit with opinions on almost everything from the state of ping pong in China to the global injustice towards short men and tall women.

William's understanding of economics left much to be desired, but his banking background was enough to persuade his party and the electorate, of his fiscal competence. His unwillingness to accept scientific advice on the impact of animal farming on climate change and environmental damage was still a popular point of view shared by many of the electorate. When the English ladies' football team, the Lionesses, all declared that they were all vegan for their health and agility and were supporting Macmillan's policy on climate change, it swayed many voters.

A dog-loving, aging pop star, Harry Stiles, a man who once had been my musical hero, called for compassion towards animals and reflected that there is little difference between his "best friend" and a farm animal so we should support a party that was concerned to eliminate animal farming. That was the Conservative party. Macmillan's pension policy had already secured support from the older voters. He finally ensured popular support amongst the young through his commitment to abandon the university fees that had been imposed on students for the last fifty years. Macmillan announced a new Bank Holiday to celebrate women's football in a popular move to distract attention from the sex scandal.

Crowd-pleasing measures secured his re-election and allowed the less popular, but more important, changes that the Conservative government planned. The continuity of government was good for my share portfolio. For many years' shares had enjoyed exceptional growth but, unknown to me, there was a shock just around the corner.

As one of the first one hundred members of the Planet for Pleasure Initiative, I was invited to a reception at Buckingham Palace to celebrate a milestone for the organisation.

Prince George, Prince of Wales, announced that his charity had reached the one million hectares target, promised seven years earlier. Cycle trails, running tracks, wild water swimming lakes, and campsites were operational in all areas of the UK. Many traditional animal species had been re-introduced to the wild and were thriving, keeping a better balance of nature. They prevented the overpopulation of squirrels and deer that had been such a threat. Due to the popularity of the scheme, he planned to double the area in the next ten years.

At his side, stood Sir Christopher Packham, the ninety-one-years-old naturalist and wildlife campaigner, and Professor Edward Winters the long-established English vegan activist from Harvard University. Both were members of the managing committee. Packham praised The Duke of Wales for the return of many "lost" species and the renewal of wildlife habitat. Edward Winters claimed that closer access to nature had improved human mental health and that the recognition of what could be achieved without animal agriculture had encouraged plant-based diets.

More than half the UK population enjoyed a wholly plant-based diet. Meat, fish, and dairy consumption in the UK was only forty percent of the level at the turn of the century despite the growth in the UK population. He called for the government to ban imported meat and fish and to withdraw any remaining subsidies to animal farmers, now that a majority of voters considered the absence of animal rights to be morally unjustified. The movement was growing and the UK was leading the way.

The production of plant-based foods was accelerated in the UK by the increase in vertical farming financed by the big food producers. Nestle, Hershey, Mars, Coca-Cola, and Kraft Heinz had all made very substantial investments in high-rise buildings in city centres where they could grow crops in controlled environments close to their markets.

Sustainable growing provided the UK with food security and had been heavily backed by the UK government subsidies. With cheap energy readily available from the wind, sun, and tidal flows and the maximisation of water usage, vertical farming has proved a great commercial success. In the UK the concentration of population and supportive planning laws gave the UK an international lead in this technology. As the big business capital investment strategy switched, the resistance to change had dwindled.

Chapter 33

I must pause my story to just remember Georgina for a few minutes. She brought colour into my life and taught me compassion. She enabled me to be the self I wanted to be. She showed a life away from the clank of cut glass Champagne flutes and the sharp edges of diamond rings. She demonstrated that kindness and empathy don't demand a handsome face or an expensive watch.

Only with Georgina did I feel comfortable with my sexuality, assured that my life had a purpose less defined by selfishness. If there is an afterlife there are a few people I 'd hope to avoid, but I hope that I meet Georgina again. She will kill me if I don't mention our wedding, that is if she can kill me when I'm already dead.

I'd arranged our wedding as quickly as I could and confessed to not wanting to risk Georgina changing her mind. It was a winter wedding in early January, a small but smart affair on a dry sunny day. My divorce had been finalised easily as Caitlin wanted to marry Aurora now that same-sex marriage was at last acceptable to her Chinese masters. We had no children, no property to dispose of, and each of us had significant wealth from our share dealing.

Caitlin and I would stay friends, although she was always uneasy with Georgina and was not invited to the wedding. I like to think that somehow Caitlin, who had enjoyed the social acceptance of a man at her side, was jealous of Georgina, but maybe I never really got over my love for Caitlin however much I tried to shrug it off.

Mia was my Best Man. She and Nova had arranged a stag night for me and my friends. It was in London on the night before the wedding. My only stag night was a quiet affair. Over a great meal at the newly vegan Dorchester Hotel, we all enjoyed congenial conversation, and companionable reminiscence but little banter. Josh was there, of course, with his intellectual expression, wearing a rather smart suit, disfigured by the inevitable apple in his pocket. Perhaps it was the subdued surroundings of the Dorchester Hotel, we were all too old for the excesses of youth, or maybe I had collected friends who were too concerned about the future of our planet to let their hair down.

I looked around the table and determined to keep the joy in my life despite the impending political problems and to remember that Utopia was just around the corner. Humanity had started slowly to realise the opportunities of plant-based diets, and at least half the populations around the world knew what to do and had made a start. The work of the Planet for Pleasure Initiative was inspiring the world.

Georgina looked beautiful on her wedding day, although the unaccustomed makeup and over-attention to her hair disguised the happy, fresh face and rumpled hairstyle I loved. We married at St. Mary and St.Nicholas Church, a small Norman church close to the banks of the Thames and near Georgina's parents' Henley home. Josh looked uncomfortable in his morning suit and perhaps a little nervous without an apple on hand. It was me who should have been nervous, not having reviewed Mia's speech. Our small party of 30 family and friends had a crowded wedding breakfast celebration in a nearby pub that had just been awarded a first Michelin star for its plant-based menu. This was a joyful occasion, full of the noise and bustle in the crowded accommodation. Mia spoke brilliantly, recounting my various misdeeds with a clever humour that had our guests in peals of laughter. Josh couldn't resist having his say, but his off-kilter jokes seemed clumsy after Mia's eloquence. I thought that at last my candles were burning brightly, but they would not last forever.

My parents, now in their early seventies, were at my wedding this time. Although they couldn't understand my break-up with Caitlin, as I never explained the truth, I think that they were delighted that I had found a wonderful partner in Georgina, who took care to spend time with them. I didn't know that this would be the last time I would see my father, who never even told my mother of the disease that was to bring his life to a premature end.

After a night stay at the Manoir aux Quat'Saisons, where the well-remembered Raymond Blanc's plant-based recipes still dominated the kitchen, we travelled for our honeymoon in Cumbria. In January we anticipated rain in the Lake District, but we were welcomed by Spring-like sunshine, blue skies, and crisp, cool days.

The Lake District had changed since my boyhood visit with my parents. The extreme weather events had eroded the many footpaths and walkways, and even in January, the hillsides were busy with tourists escaping the hot weather in Central Europe. We stayed at the Langdale Chase Hotel, a magnificent Victorian house on the shores of Lake Windermere, that had been a hotel for more than 100 years. The days lacked the cold winter mornings that I remembered from my youth, but the views retained the spectacular promise of February springtime, with the heathers already in bud.

We walked endlessly, often with nothing to say, but with a comfortable quietness whilst our hearts sang out at the beauty of the lakes. Seen from the hillside, the water was a misleadingly clear green. Closer inspection revealed that algae pollution had changed the water. Rugged hills, shale climbs, and January cool all worked together to make a memorable holiday in a special county, but everywhere there were the signs of coming changes.

I remember the visit mostly for our long breakfasts together as we faced each day as though it was the first day of our lives together. Now I could not imagine a life without my new wife, but that is what I would face eventually.

Georgina and I bought a house together. It was my first ever real home. I was approaching fifty and for only the econd time, I had my own place of refuge from the world. Book sales were continuing as my story had been converted into seventy-five different languages, and sales had topped eight million copies. The book was still selling as readers gazed into my future and their prospective time ahead. I kept planning my second book but, to the exasperation of my publisher, I found that I had little more to say.

We had paid two million pounds for a little Georgian cottage in need of renovation, set in four acres of Surrey Hills' woodland near my parent's home and not far from Nova and Mia in Farnham. Georgina could see the potential in a way I never could and immediately set about discussions with architects, engineers, and planners. In a little over a year, the house was remodelled into a home that retained the heritage, patina, and period features but became a warm and spacious place where we could find quiet comfort.

Georgina was away a lot continuing her career by seeking out locations for documentaries. So often the location came first and the documentary followed, as documentary makers recorded the loss of human habitat and the destruction of the planet. I was comfortable in my solitude with long country walks, workouts in my private gym, swimming in the outdoor pool, and always with something in the garden in need of my attention.

I had time to read and research like never before, and I became obsessed with the news channels. The Earth's temperature was still rising, although the rate of growth had slowed very marginally. The target tipping point of one point seven five degrees had long been surpassed, but climate model simulations now believed it could be held at two degrees above pre-industrial levels. Everybody would feel as though they lived 600 miles nearer the Equator than in the same location at the turn of the century. Even if this revised prediction were to be realised and temperature rises contained, it would be devastating for so many people.

After weeks of worry and little sleep, I again realised that I must do what I could to prevent this disaster. The world needed America and China to champion rewilding and speed up the rate of change. I decided to travel to Washington to plead for change. I booked the flight, but my plan was to be delayed by something even more important to me.

Chapter 34

I have made all the arrangements for my funeral and even sent the invitations. I don't expect many to attend. My surviving old friends won't want to travel, and I don't want the recipients of my charitable work to attend just to find out if they are mentioned in my will. There is just one person I really would like to be there, and I am still hoping that he will come here later in the day to see me off.

Talking of my funeral reminds me of my father. It was a sunny day for his funeral, but all I felt was the guilt of not having seen my parents in almost a year. My father had not mentioned his prostate cancer, even to my mother, until he was taken into the hospital only two days before he died. I had been unable to see him. We only learnt from the doctors that it had been diagnosed in September 2050 when his cancer was already untreatable.

The treatment that had cured my Mum 25 years earlier had been unsuccessful for my father. The doctors were amazed that he had carried on so long. We thought that his aching bones, tiredness, and even the swelling in his legs were just symptoms of old age. I was astonished that he had not shared the bad news.

At my wedding, he knew he was dying and carried the burden of that knowledge alone to save us all from sharing the worry. He had quietly put his affairs in good order and left a long list of instructions for me and Mum, written several months ago. I was as proud of Dad at his funeral as I was in awe of him on my fourth birthday when he comforted me whilst others laughed over the four red trick candles.

Georgina was a great support to me, my sisters, and mostly my mother, and we celebrated his life with the many friends he had made in the railways and the local cricket club, where he had umpired until the end of last season.

I learnt a lot about my father that I never understood in his lifetime. It turned out that the rather quiet man I had known was something of a joker with his friends and business colleagues. He had turned a blind eye when ruling on an LBW decision against our village batsman, but hardly any LBW appeals were rejected when his village team was bowling. After a short but miserable stint in banking, he had spent nearly all his career in the railways. Father had retired as a senior railways manager who was well respected by his colleagues. He had been known as "the Controller" in memory of some children's television program broadcast when he started in 2008, maybe because he was always a little overweight. He was respected for giving important staff talks in rhythm and was famous for his Christmas party odes to his staff. I couldn't get out of my head the nonsense limerick my father had so often repeated to me at bath time:

"There was a young man from Surrey

Who feasted on Indian curry

His tummy ballooned out in a bump

Then back with a loud, smelly trump

Which distressed all the people of Surrey"

I felt an overwhelming sadness and an unexpected emptiness realising that I had never really known my father. I only met the version of himself that he presented to his only son. I learnt too late of his readiness for fun and mischievous personality. Knowing it gave me a new freedom, safe in the knowledge that he would not disapprove of my more reckless moments.

Chapter 35

It's a long time ago now but my father's life and distant companionship became more important to me after he died. I hope my life becomes as important to someone when I have died. It's only the little things that bring back memories of the dead and I so want to be remembered for big things. I can't think of anything worthwhile that I have achieved despite my best intentions.

My father's untimely death left me with a new sense of loneliness. Although I had seen little of him and usually my mother had dominated our metacalls, I had always known he was there and on my side. My very capable mother seemed to be taking her change in circumstances calmly and I decided that I should pursue my ambition to influence climate change by going to America.

With Georgina committed to visiting Nigeria for a documentary, I set off for Washington to see Hendrix. I stayed at the New Willard Hotel and it brought back many memories. I was sure that I could get to see President Jackson Hendrix James. I was confident that he would want to meet up with his friend of six years ago, but it wasn't to be. However, it was a meeting by chance with his young protege, Jane Willis, that proved so productive.

Jane Willis, successor to the President as Senator for Massachusetts, was an obviously powerful woman of a similar age to me. We were introduced by Henry, the barman at the New Willard, as sharing similar interests. Jane was small and dark, I imagine Indian heritage although I never asked, with big white teeth and an ample figure. She was a busy woman with a rather loud voice, unable to relax, her eyes always searching the room. She had read my life story in *The Future Past of an Extraordinary Man* and wanted to engage with me about how we could avert the dangers of global warming. She agreed that the reduction in fossil fuel usage and the limited carbon capture facilities were insufficient to prevent the climate disaster.

Jane knew that animal agriculture contributed very significantly to greenhouse gas emissions and other unsustainable environmental damage. She was also convinced by *Diet for Peace* the early century writings of Dr Will Tuttle who had died recently aged 98. Tuttle argued we could not be a peaceful society whilst slaughtering animals and that kindness and understanding come from the less aggressive plant-based diet.

Violence on your plate had encouraged acceptance of violence generally. But how could anyone convince red-blooded Americans that roasting animal flesh over the barbecue was not an essential of life?

Jane and I giggled together over too many cocktails and joked about how she would change the American way when she became the fiftieth President of the USA and appointed me her climate advisor. Jane was a lot smarter than me and rather shy and reserved when she was sober, but after two dry martinis, she was fun and a good listener. Maybe I just believed that after I too had enjoyed a couple of dry martinis. We spent most evenings together debating how she could achieve such a change, with me never believing that she might one day get the chance to test our wild ideas.

The ideas were silly. Could we stop the cattle ranching by outlawing cowboy boots and battered Stetson hats? Could we ban the manufacture of slaughterhouse knives? Could we impose an impossibly high tax on the blood-swilling pressure hoses? We speculated that all abattoirs should have a priest to read the last rites to each animal to be killed and to oversee their funerals. We wondered if only laboratory-grown meat could be labelled as pork, ham or bacon that pig should be called pig and that cow should be labelled cow, not beef or steak. How could we ban meat production or separate an American man from his burger? Raising taxes on animal products would slow demand but make food expensive and the responsible politician unelectable.

Perhaps we would have to wait until the prairies had finally dried out completely and the soil turned to fruitless dust like the Dust Bowl of the Great Plains in the 1930s, but this time with no hope of a rain-filled recovery. When there was little hope, and only starving herds of cattle left, the American people would realise their folly.

I told Jane of the mood swings that were impacting the UK. Especially the elderly were more aware of the dangerous planet they had bequeathed to their children and grandchildren, as a result of their short-sighted selfishness. Maybe the time had come, to be honest with the electorate and to rely on their good sense, raise taxes and be damned.

I never flirted with Jane or her with me. Our holiday friendship had been about two lonely people, away from home, concerned for the planet, musing about what could and should be done. My trip to Washington was a failure as President James seemed to have forgotten me. If his researchers had explained my book, he may have felt annoyed by my claim to have influenced his inaugural speech or just embarrassed that he had abandoned some of his principles in favour of expediency. Either way, I was disappointed that I had no influence over American policy, although in this I was mistaken.

Chapter 36

The Portuguese Laurel hedge outside my study window needs cutting. I should have replaced Peter with a more modern version that can perform these outdoor tasks but, somehow, I have become accustomed to his scowl. It would be unkind to send him for scrap. Maintaining the garden is a job I will never have to do again. There are many little tasks that I have complained about, but now I can only see the pleasure in them. I've had more than my allotted time, but I'm not ready to go. There is so much to see, to smell, to wonder about and to fill one with optimism.

I returned to England from Washington in a hurry to see Georgina on her return from Nigeria. Jane Willis was soon a happy but distant memory. I was so pleased to be back in my bed with the beautiful Georgina. Georgina had been researching the aftermath of the 2049 floods and landslides in Lagos, home to fifteen million Nigerians and part of the growing megalopolis stretching six hundred miles along the West African coastline where three hundred million Africans live in squalid shanty towns, vulnerable to the changing weather patterns, rising sea levels and coastal erosion.

On her return home, Georgina couldn't sleep. Her experience in Nigeria had left her traumatised. She could only explain how different the tragedy was in reality, compared to the horrific, but sterilised, images on the

Metaverse news feeds. Two years after the floods and landslides that had killed nearly fifty thousand citizens and destroyed so much more, there was little sign of recovery and so much remaining evidence of the disaster. Mud-filled roads impossible to clear, broken buildings beyond repair, poverty, buckled drains, unhealed injury and disability, shanty towns, starvation, the smell and sounds of unwashed humanity fighting for survival in a climate of torrential rains and stifling heat, were locked in her memory. Even after the massive vaccination programme, malaria was endemic as the warm humid climate encouraged the multiplication of mosquitos that brought the disease in from the rural inland areas in vast numbers. Evidence of nausea and diarrhea were unhidden. With yellowing skin and eyes, people tried helplessly to look cheerful despite their hopeless predicament.

Lack of food and water and the unchecked spread of disease were still shattering families and dismantling relationships among the survivors. Charity workers and the few remaining public services were tired by the futility of their efforts and frustrated that the world had forgotten their plight as news media moved on to the next disaster.

The climate crisis was not about numbers on a page, not about degrees warmer or megatons of CO_2 emissions, not even about the economic changes, or the collapse of tourism caused by disappearing beaches. Nor was it about the disappearance of productive farmland due to overheating and coastal erosion. The climate crisis was about people, about starvation, depravation, poverty and pain. Climate change caused rising water levels, disease, mud slides, destruction and despair. It had already destroyed communities, dispersed families and dismantled centuries-old ways of life.

Georgina felt despair at her inability to influence the change that was so damaging for so many of those less fortunate in society. I could not console her. I told Georgina about Senator Jane Willis and her ambition for change in America. My book *The Future Past of an Extraordinary Man* had been made into a very successful film you may have seen and, from the proceeds, we decided to offer Jane Willis one million dollars towards her Presidential campaign if she would agree to put her name forward and promote her message of dietary change for Americans, still the biggest consumers on the planet. At least we were doing something, but it was not enough to help Georgina escape the memories that tormented her. The fun-loving energetic person I had married was now filled with despair, resenting the human species that had done so much damage, unable to face the magnitude of the world's problems and unwilling to celebrate the small achievements made.

Chapter 37

Georgina refused medical help for her depression and never found an optimism that could have helped her escape her concern for the people of Nigeria. Her natural empathy ensured that she would always be thinking about the hardships faced by so many nations because of the human-induced climate crisis. If only Georgina had found some optimism, she and I would have had so much more happiness.

How I wish that I had been able to show Georgina the kinder and happier place the world has now become. It's nearly 4:00pm and time for the News Report I usually watch. It's hard to be interested in the news when you know that tomorrow you will play no part in the future. My visitor has not arrived. Maybe if he comes it will only be because of his expected inheritance. I've met a lot of people who have made lots of money and many of them have put it to good use. All of us end up dead, as I will be tomorrow. Society needs wealth creators, but it all seems so pointless when death beckons.

I was at home when I learnt that Maxim Devin, the manager of the Mandarin Oriental Hotel in Moscow, had sold land in Siberia to a Chinese consortium for a staggering two billion dollars. He had been quietly buying frozen land in Siberia in the expectation that climate change would release the potential. The unexpected demand from China had pushed prices beyond his expectations and made him a massive profit. Land purchased for five hundred dollars per hectare early in the century was now selling for five thousand dollars per hectare and Maxim's modest investment had made him a billionaire. Anastas, his son, my travel guide for the day in Moscow, would now be able to finance his political ambition.

Politics in Russia were still confusing. Following the democratic election of President Pavel Pasternak the Russian United Party had followed a Putin-style authoritarian rule, but without the support of Putin's oligarch friends. Unable to force his ideas on a frustrated population and lacking the ruthlessness of Putin, he resigned from his position after street protests about the falling living standards and increasing Chinese influence. Russia had failed to gain its place in the world during the twelve years of leadership of Pasternak due to the corruption and endless bureaucracy that was systemic in the Russian government.

Anastas was a leading figure in the new Democratic Liberal Party who had won power on a landslide of popular opinion. However, the process of government was much harder than the campaign to be elected. Siberia, secretly supported by China, was demanding independence. Investigations into the financial ties between members of the government and crime cartels were so all-encompassing that many of the institutions of state were implicated. Even the Ladies' football team was accused of match-fixing.

The improved relations with the West were sagging under the uncertainty. Economic progress was slow despite the potential wealth unlocked by climate change. From the comfort of my home, I wondered if Russia would ever break free of the duplicity that appeared to be a national characteristic, but I believed that Anastas would be a force for good. I hoped that his father's new wealth would be put to good use and eventually, it was.

Chapter 38

Cricket is my favourite sport. The intellectual challenge of bowling to a selected field placement competes with the excitement and courage of the individual batter, but it is rugby that I turn to with my next memory and the end of rugby union as a professional sport.

I had been invited to the Calcutta Cup, the first rugby match in the Seven Nations Cup. Scotland came to Twickenham to play England for what proved to be the final time. After the traditional, rather boozy, picnic lunch in the car park, we took our seats in the stadium as part of a rowdy but good-tempered crowd with supporters of each side evenly matched in the sound of their support, if not in numbers.

The heavily padded players took to the field wearing the lightweight head protection that had been mandatory for the last twenty years. The on-field contests were ferocious as each side fought for dominance and the walking wounded were replaced at half time with England fifteen points to six ahead.

Scotland scored a try shortly after the restart, bringing them within one score of a victory. The match was abandoned after sixty-four minutes. A head clash between England's twenty-two years old back, Jonny Graham, and Scotland's captain, Bill Robertson, left them both with serious injuries. Jonny Graham died on the pitch. The euphoria of the pulsating game, encouraged by my lunchtime alcohol, left me in an instant as the shock of seeing the life of a young athlete stolen from him in pursuit of a meaningless victory. I think that all the one hundred thousand supporters in the stadium realised that rugby had become too violent and too risky for the huge, powerful men who played at this highest level.

Because junior players only played the less popular form of tag rugby, young senior players had little experience of the brutalism of international rugby galvanised by nationalistic, patriotic crowds. All attempts at head protection had failed and the international organisers had no option but to ban further matches to await the outcome of the Coroner's report.

The Coroner held that the RFU was responsible, creating the possibility of a manslaughter charge against the organisation and leaving World Rugby unable to obtain insurance. It was these changes that brought the professional game to an end. This was the last time the Calcutta Cup was contested after one hundred and seventy-two years.

I felt sorry that the continuity of experience would be lost, I could only celebrate that common sense had outlawed a game that had become so ruthlessly savage that it could hardly be called a sport. Although I would miss the spectacle, I was glad that rugby union had followed the lead of boxing, that had banned the professional sport eight years earlier.

Chapter 39

Do all we older people look back on the adventures of our youth and claim, "It was better when I was young"? I regret the end of professional rugby as the professionals led the way and the whole game has been in decline since that awful day, but I wouldn't have wanted my son to play. Change is not always progress, but safety must take priority over sport.

Achievements can be found in many activities. I desired to achieve something important and to help Georgina escape the demons that haunted her after she visited Nigeria, which took me on a frustrating visit to China.

Georgina travelled with me to Beijing, where we stayed at the Aman at the Summer Palace for a true Chinese experience. The hotel, built in traditional style, was like a time machine. It is built within the East Gate of the magnificent Summer Palace that sits in a vast area of lakes and gardens. The hotel is simply decorated in the Ming dynasty style, with furnishings emphasising the feeling of calm and a step back in time.

In the Summer Palace Georgina could relax, walk in the courtyard and palace grounds, take a spa and escape her frustration and melancholy. I hoped to renew old acquaintances from my time in Shanghai and encourage a change in Chinese policy towards animal farming. I expected to be received by the powerful people I had met at the Jin Jiang Hotel in Shanghai and in that I wasn't totally disappointed.

China had taken big steps towards improving the terrible air pollution that had plagued all industrial towns in the early part of the century by shifting from coal power to natural gas. An extensive program of renewable energy was underway. Authorities had clamped down on polluting factories and old petrol or diesel cars. They had planted five million trees in a programme designed to offset carbon emissions. They had built almost 1000 plastic reclamation facilities, one in every city or town. This had not been enough to halt China, still, the biggest producer and user of plastics, from being overwhelmed with unwanted waste.

The population of China had settled at one and a half billion people, more than twenty percent of the world's population. As prosperity grew from the ingenuity of the people and the foresight of the government's investment programme, so did the demands for a Western lifestyle. The infant democracy created a new short-term legislative programme. Demand for meat and dairy products could not be controlled and politicians still turned their head against the scientific evidence of the contribution of animal farming to greenhouse gas emissions for fear of losing voters.

The farming towers were high-rise, industrialised animal compounds. They were seen everywhere and were used to house pigs in crates for pork commodity production and cows for dairy milk. The Chinese Government showed little regard for the health of the nation and no regard for farm animal welfare. The controlled animal environment and new measures to dispose of excrement and displace methane provided a misplaced excuse to embrace the multi-storey, pasture-less fields of animal misery.

Fenhua Li, who I had met several times at the Jin Jiang Hotel in Shanghai, was still the President of China until the next election, due in 2054. She agreed to see me at her residence in Zhongnanhai, the compound, adjacent to the famous hidden city, that still housed the state leaders. I was treated with polite formality. I made my case for a rethink of Chinese farming policy to help avoid the devastating floods and storms that were already battering the shores of China, improve health outcomes for all and end food poverty. I asked her to reconsider if farm animals deserved more compassionate treatment. I explained that such a policy might appeal to the rapidly ageing population. Fenhua Li, through her interpreter, politely thanked me, and said that it was under consideration, but she was not ready to take the electoral risk involved. I hope that her re-election would provide the time and opportunity for an essential but unpopular policy.

I sought out Mingze Wang the opposition leader, but he couldn't or wouldn't meet me. I looked for activists who could carry the message, but the Chinese still had an accepting mentality and a reluctance for rebellion. I had failed to bring the hope I had felt in England to the planet's major polluter.

I did, however, enjoy a few memorable days with Georgina. In Beijing, we strolled through the much larger than I expected Tiananmen Square, and, in the continuing smog, admired the recently erected memorial to the hundreds of students who died in the 1989 massacre. It was warm and damp as we walked with many other sightseers around the traditional buildings in the Forbidden City, built by the 1406 Ming Emperor of China. We also walked a section of the Great Wall and visited Jingshan Park, but our favourite moments were close to the hotel in the beautiful grounds of the Summer Palace.

The beauty of the past raised Georgina's spirits. The Halls of Happiness and the Garden of Harmonious Pleasure were insufficient for a lasting change and Georgina soon fell back to the despair of humankind that she believed was relentlessly destroying much of the essential habitat through warfare, overconsumption, overpopulation, pollution and an unsustainable diet. I failed to encourage her with words about our progress in the increase in renewable forms of energy, reduction of greenhouse gasses, re-wilding projects and the restoration of forests through large-scale tree planting schemes. Georgina would never find the joy in her life that surely she deserved.

Chapter 40

After our return from China, we nearly lost the home that Georgina had so lovingly created. If anything was going to reinforce her melancholy was losing our home. Nothing prepared me for fire and the threat it imposes when it's at your doorstep.

A summer hot spell in the UK usually meant temperatures in the low forty degrees Celsius, but in July 2053, temperatures peaked at forty-seven degrees and the heatwave continued for six weeks. The woodland pine trees of the Surrey Hills were dry tinder when the fire was started by an errant barbecue and the whole area was soon a raging furnace of burning timber.

One hundred square miles of ancient woodland was lost as the fire jumped fire breaks, crossed roads and showed no respect for the thousand firefighters working tirelessly to bring it under control. The habitat of many wild species was destroyed over the eight days of relentless spread of fire and 198 homes were destroyed or damaged. The lives of three firefighters were lost.

Our home was intact, scorched and smoke-damaged but otherwise untouched in spite of it being close to the woodland. Dousing it with water from the swimming pool and the removal of trees close to the buildings had helped us survive A last-minute change in the wind direction had saved our home and with it all the memories it already held for us. The fear remained with the knowledge that all could be lost so easily.

The process of restoration began again as smoke-damaged rooms were re-decorated, but Georgina had lost her enthusiasm and our restoration lost the charm and excitement of our earlier changes. I haven't redecorated since. At the time the tiredness of our surroundings seemed to reflect the general decline of our bodies and softening of our hopes as we passed the fifty years milestone. But I was far from finished.

Chapter 41

Twilight turns to darkness outside but the story of my life and the 21st Century had surprises and excitements still to come. I still had a close interest in politics in America and my old friend Hendrix would be replaced by my new acquaintance Jane Willis.

President Jackson Hendrix James' second term in office had come to an end. He had been a popular leader. His endorsement of Jane Willis, the Democratic candidate, ensured her election as his successor.

A Republican majority in the Senate would prevent any controversial legislation, but Jane Willis had campaigned to retain the kindness policy championed by President James. His two terms in office had initiated some important developments in the American way of life, but the high ideals had been scaled back and the results had been disappointing.

The Supreme Court had ruled that his gun control policies were unconstitutional. His Executive Order to stop police and government officials from routinely carrying guns had prevailed, as had greater punishment for gun crime.

The outlawing of automatic weapons and a zero-tolerance policy have resulted in less gun violence among criminal gangs. The change in gun culture awareness has discouraged gun ownership, particularly among the young. Nevertheless, mass killings continued, perpetuated by the publicity given to the deranged combatants.

President James' plea for kindness had encouraged a change to a music culture of peace, affection and tenderness that, in turn, engendered a gentle society priding courtesy and decency. The US was better regarded around the World and political changes in Israel and China were seen as positive successes of the James administration.

The education policy had received quiet approval and got off to a stuttering start, but was now bringing old and young to an easier understanding and, surprisingly, encouraging a revival of late twentieth-century music. The community projects were a resounding success from the start and were shown to improve worker productivity and reduce employment churn, as well as giving a new emphasis to community cohesion and crime reduction.

The food policy was not such a success. There was a great deal of resistance to President James' dietary demands and not all States had adopted the policy of plant-based meals in public buildings, schools, universities and hospitals despite the Federal Law. Big dairy companies had bought the new microbe milk producers and suppressed retail sales, although microbe milk was extensively used in food manufacture, especially in the making of chocolate.

Further health studies and the need to demonstrate the means of food production from farm to fork had persuaded a growing number of people to follow a plant-based diet, but the burger chains still sold more meat burgers than the plant-based alternatives. The anticipated reduction in obesity levels and better health outcomes had not materialised.

Campaigning to the better educated, more considerate, sympathetic electorate that had responded to President Jame's pleas for kindness and seen national and international acceptance, Jane Willis had promised to reduce animal farming by withdrawing subsidies, increasing taxation and imposing higher welfare standards on an industry that was already feeling the consequences of poor pasture and soil erosion.

Abattoirs and slaughterhouses would be separately categorised and suffer a special property tax to reflect the pollution they cause. Animal products would become unaffordable except for the wealthy. She would set up a re-wilding project based on the Prince of Wales's Planet for Pleasure Initiative in the UK.

The decline in animal agriculture would help tackle the world food crisis because grain and soya production would now be used to feed the human population rather than the farmed animals. These changes in the food supply chain would correct the food distribution patterns that had caused the starvation of poor communities, now made worse by the impact of global warming.

The subsidy policy changes and the new dietary demands

had been a massive risk for Jane Willis in the swing states of the Midwest, but the retired population of the sunshine belt, with their concern for their grandchildren, had given their wholehearted support and Florida, Georgia, Nevada and Pennsylvania had all voted Jane Willis into the Whitehouse.

Jane Willis had connected with the growing number of retired voters who had become the dominant electorate in America and, as President, she would continue to respond to and rely on these elderly constituents.

I sent Jane Willis, the fiftieth President of the USA, a bottle of gin and my favourite martini recipe (add an olive) with my card of congratulations, but I wasn't surprised that the formal thanks I received did not include the promised invitation to be Secretary of State for Climate.

COP 64 October 2058 Moscow, Russia

Moscow hosted the COP *64 virtual conference.*

The temperature was two degrees above pre-industrial levels The tipping point had been passed. Ice melt had reduced solar reflection. Permafrost in the tundra of North America and Russian Siberia was retreating, releasing natural CO2 deposits. Sea levels had risen 70cm and would continue to rise for thousands of years.

The world population had risen to 10 billion. The oceans were almost empty of fish. The world was at last recognising that animal farming was unsustainable. Breeding and rearing of farm animals had been severely reduced. The number of land animals slaughtered annually for food had been halved since the 2045 peak, although it was still a staggering 50 billion animals each year.

Chapter 42

Has my chair got harder or my bottom bonier? I've been sitting here too long. My story isn't nearly finished. Perhaps a cup of tea or maybe a strong beer for old times' sake as I recall my visit to Germany. There was no hiding from the impact of climate change by the middle of the century. Life in Europe had changed, as had been forecast by climatologists, but in ways that we hadn't been willing to accept at the beginning of the century.

Nova and Mia invited Georgina and me to Stuttgart, Germany, to celebrate the purchase of The Mercedes Motor Company by Jaguar Land Rover. The automobile factories in Germany were now fully automated and electric convey cars were mass-produced in staggering numbers. Industry in the Ruhr Valley had been destroyed by the rising sea levels and new industries had been built in the Stuttgart region. Germany was no longer the industrial powerhouse of the early century as heavy industry had fallen into decline.

A lack of initiative and an unwillingness to supplement oil and solar power with nuclear energy had slowed Germany's economy. It had been further damaged by the impact of rising sea levels on the main industrial regions in the Rhine Valley. This fall in values enabled Jaguar Land Rover to make a strategic purchase at an opportune moment and I was glad that Mia had encouraged me to include shares in Mercedes in my portfolio.

The reception was held in the enormous industrial unit that housed the production line of the Mercedes electric convey car. The fully automated production line required only two operators and five support engineers. It produced fifteen thousand convey cars each day when running at maximum capacity. Almost a thousand people attended the party and Mia provided a rousing speech about international cooperation, the return of Jaguar to transport vehicle production and the opportunities in Europe for the Jaguar housing pods.

It all appeared to me to be the moment that the UK's independence from the European Union had at last paid dividends and that the UK was once again a leading industrial nation.

Chapter 43

It's now time for a cup of tea. Beer is not part of Peter's programmed response. He has disappeared to make tea at the regular time of 5:00 pm. At least our English habit of tea at 5 o'clock has endured. While he has gone let me tell you about my visit to Mexico.

I had never been so happy as when Georgina and I decided to holiday in Mexico City. I felt sure that a visit to one of the world's most vibrant cities would propel her out of the depression she had experienced since her visit to Nigeria. For a while it did. I had never visited Central America and looked forward to the energetic hustle and bustle of one of the world's most talked about cities.

Georgina was doing some early scouting for a new film and it provided the incentive we needed to visit Mexico City. After we had booked into the Four Seasons Hotel, Georgina, who had done her research for the film, was the perfect guide, bringing her beauty, intelligence and enthusiasm to every situation. We visited the tourist traps to see Chapultepec Castle, The Museo del Templo Mayor and Cathedral Metrópolitana la Ciudad de Mexico and we marvelled at the ancient history.

There was no Opera available, but we listened to the Mexico National Symphony Orchestra play Mozart's Symphony no 41 and Beethoven's symphony no 5 in the amazing Palacio de Bellas Artes. Georgina was overwhelmed with the emotion of the music, but the aching beauty did little to lighten her mood. Events in Mexico only magnified her problems.

Our best times were roaming the streets and sampling the tacos from the street stalls. We also ate in the famous Pugol restaurant, where the family Olivera still created dishes from the Spanish gastronomic heritage in fine style. Georgina and I drank rather too much Mezcal, a smoky drink like Tequila, a happy drink that matched our mood.

The Mezcal left little appetite for the rather ordinary wine from the Casa Madero vineyard that followed. Later, I found that Casa Madero had been producing wine since 1597 and I wondered why they hadn't yet quite mastered the art, although my taste buds may have been dulled by the Mezcal that had preceded the meal.

June was still the best time to visit Mexico, with average temperatures in the late 20 degrees. The days were hot and the evenings warmed like a velvet cape. Air pollution from the seven million vehicles that contested the streets was still a problem.

Many old petrol and diesel vehicles noisily filled the streets despite the renewable energy units installed across the city in public and private buildings. Pollution was reduced in June as the high winds cleared the air. The real hurricane season was not yet upon us, but the climate was changing and we did experience an unexpected storm of a ferocity I hadn't seen before.

We were sitting in Parque Nacional El Tepeyac overlooking the vast city when the skies darkened, winds increased, and the heavy rain tumbled out of the clouds like a wave crashing on the seashore. I would have been drier standing fully clothed in the shower and as the rain flattened Georgina's hair and made her clothes transparent, I could only marvel at her beauty. Now nearly 60, Georgina still had the figure of a teenager with small, firm breasts and a slim waist and hips. With the rain pouring over us, I took her in my embrace and gave her a kiss I still remember as we giggled about our predicament like two teenagers in an illicit moment.

Although our plight was a time of bliss for us, it brought tragedy for many of the 10 million residents of Mexico City. That day 100mm of rain fell in just 12 hours. The inadequate drainage could not cope with almost one month's rain in half a day.

Intensive development had concreted so much of the area that little or no water reached the underground aquifers and water shortages would continue despite the flooding. Street trash left in the city was swept towards the drains by the flood water and then further blocked the drains, preventing the water from escaping.

Much of the city was underwater and even the Four Seasons Hotel suffered water damage on the ground floor reception areas, kitchens and cellars. Mexico was vulnerable to the impact of climate change because of the geographical situation.

The smell of sewage was everywhere, and the crowded housing areas seemed full of despairing citizens up to their thighs in water, sometimes carrying a child, always with a numb expression of horror and disappointment at what they had lost. Eventually, the floods would subside. The streets would be washed clean of the effluent and debris left behind, but the flooding waters carried away the household memories and ambitions of so many people who faced the constant threat of repetition.

Once again Georgina could not hide from the memories of Nigeria now reinforced by this sad new experience. As the pictures of so much human pain filled our minds, we returned home to the Surrey Hills, hoping that similar conditions wouldn't occur in the stable UK.

Chapter 44

Digestive biscuits seem to have weathered every storm unchanged. They are so welcome with a cup of tea. I like the crisp taste of the biscuit. Peter is programmed to be in control of my nutrition, but it surely doesn't matter now. I will send him for an extra biscuit while I update you on American politics.

2061 was time for another election in America and Jane Willis, having completed two terms, would be standing down. I was home in England when I learnt that President Jane Willis had been largely condemned by a newly nationalistic media in America for the accommodating international policies she had pursued. Social media still provided a level of scrutiny and criticism that made the process of government more difficult each year.

Media needed controversy and created gossip to provide it and conversation that, in turn, encouraged businesses to advertise. Advertising was still the lifeblood of the media. Big animal food production businesses had railed against the changes that Jane had implemented.

Even the pharmaceutical industry giants put their weight behind promotions to encourage milk and beef consumption in the light of evidence that a plant-based diet was reducing the nation's demand for medication. Jane supported the new Democratic candidate, Paul Bryson, but he had little chance of electoral success when his Republican rival declared against the restrictions imposed by President Willis.

The republican candidate Hank Brennan assumed office as the fifty-first President of the United States of America. President Jane Willis had achieved a peaceful transition towards a kinder society during her two terms of office, but the American electorate felt that she had been too soft on the Chinese territorial ambition. China had bought heavily into the poorer countries of Africa, where the Chinese investments had bought substantial influence, if not control, over a large part of the region.

China was now investing in Siberia and a hidden influence in the separatist campaign there that would further disrupt western unity. In his inaugural speech, Hank Brennan promised a new toughness and claimed that kindness was not working in international affairs. I wondered how the gains of the last 25 years could be discarded so easily. His domestic policy was largely unchanged as his options were limited by a Democratic majority in the House of Representatives and the Senate.

Chapter 45

I have always talked to Josh, although we saw little of each other except on the screen. I had been the best man for his first wedding, but it had failed, childless and painfully. I never quite realised why he was so attractive to women, but he had quickly married again to Ava, a much younger wife. I was a little envious of his two small children, but he assured me that they were more work than pleasure.

I was amazed to hear his name headlining the news on all media outlets. He appeared peering through his large spectacles in a crumpled suit, bulging at the pocket with the unavoidable apple. He was explaining evidence that messages had been received from another planet.

A pattern of intermittent rays of light issued 1500 years ago from Kepler has been received and analysed. Experts had been unable to decipher the message to establish the meaning. It was clearly more than a random set of information.

At last, this was proof of another civilisation in the planetary system. Josh, sponsored by AT&T, had been working on the project for many years despite the lack of investment in space travel. Perhaps this realisation that other civilisations exist would spark a new surge in space probes.

I wondered what an alien civilisation would make of us here on earth. We had thought ourselves so clever but had acted to plunder our world with a selfishness that threatened to destroy our own habitat as we had already destroyed the habitat of so many creatures.

I am determined to meet up with Josh soon. Although we had kept in touch through the annual exchange of Christmas and birthday cards, we hadn't bothered to meet since my wedding. My resolve was soon forgotten, but Georgina was to come to my rescue. That wasn't the only surprise life had in store.

Chapter 46

The mug of tea was good and what little is left has gone cold. That will be me tomorrow. What little is left gone cold. My story will live on, and I hope it will record a past that must never be repeated and outline a future with so much hope. My sixtieth birthday seems a long time ago now, but it was a memorable occasion in more ways than one.

Georgina treated me with an unexpected trip back to the Sandringham Hotel for my sixtieth birthday. When I arrived, I was overwhelmed to meet some old friends, invited to my surprise party. My Mum, now in her late eighties, was holding forth in the bar with all my friends in awe of her naughty reminisces to the obvious embarrassment of my two sisters as their husbands looked on, smirking. My best friend Mia looked young, elegant and happy but Nova showed some signs of ageing since our wedding day. I was pleased to find that my little seen but constant friend, Josh was waiting to greet me. I observed his thinning hair and lined face and realised that I, too was ageing more quickly than I was ready to admit. He was still very excited about his discovery of life at some time on another planet and he carried his newfound celebrity with real modesty.

My biggest surprise was to see Bess, my university girlfriend. Georgina had found Bess through social media and persuaded her to come along. Bess was widowed. Her husband had been killed in a skiing accident in Morzine some years earlier. She came accompanied by her eldest son, Noah. I was delighted that she looked so happy and not surprised to learn that she had two other sons and a daughter. She already had two grandchildren. I felt an immediate connection with Noah, who, at thirty-eight, was comfortable in his own skin, content with his family life as a teacher of English, but ambitious to be a published author. It was Georgina who drew my attention to the physical similarities between Noah and myself. She said he walked like me, with his feet pointing at ten to two. I had never realised that I had an unusual walk. Taller than me, Noah had a similar-shaped head, unruly dark hair and a young, fresh, likeable face. He wasn't shy about telling me that he had been born in 2025. This was just a few months after the graduation day celebrations at Exeter University.

Could Noah be my son? If he is, should I tell him? As I considered the exciting possibility, the party continued.

Our Saturday night, our black-tie celebration dinner was illuminated by a tremendous lightning show and the hotel shivered under the sound of overhead thunder. Torrential rain followed and with it the prospect of flooding. We abandoned the dancing, left the staff placing sandbags at the doorways and scuttled to our first-floor bedrooms for a final drink in our suite and a midnight bedtime, somewhat earlier than planned.

When we woke the next morning, the sun was shining in a clear blue sky, but the hotel was surrounded by water as far as we could see. From our room, we didn't appreciate that it was nearly two metres deep. Power cables had been washed away, and the water supply and drainage were inoperable.

Newscasts on our Metaphones showed that the storm had coincided with a high tide and the limited coastal defences had been breached. Rising sea levels had previously eroded the coastal area, submerging the stony beaches, but now the seawater had fully engulfed Norfolk and much of Suffolk. Nearby Kings Lynn was totally submerged and the seawater spread almost 50 miles as far as Peterborough.

The university town of Cambridge was now a coastal resort. News came through of further coastal flooding in Humberside, where the sea had reached Doncaster. Sizewell Nuclear Power Station had already been closed, but decommissioning was not yet finished and fear rose of the possibility of the escape of nuclear waste.

All the effort and ambition of the re-wilding projects to create a sustainable natural habitat for our embattled wildlife in Norfolk had been destroyed overnight.

The emergency services were overwhelmed, but public appeals brought out many small boats. The sea in what was previously farmland Norfolk, was full of small crafts ferrying people to the safety of dry land many miles away. Without heating, power and water, my party were tired, a little hung over and cold. I feared for my mother, but she was the first to be rescued alongside all the lady guests. Georgina insisted on staying to the last and waiting with me and the remaining men. We had no idea if or when we would see our personal belongings left at the hotel. Our convey cars were abandoned with no chance of recovery as the sea had captured the land forever.

Our island habitat was shrinking. We, too, were amongst the planet's suffering people. Our fellow countrymen were now displaced refugees, albeit in our own country. Nobody could escape the impact of climate change, but could this be the event that finally enforced change in our behaviour? Could this awful event give us hope?

It wasn't the moment to discuss Noah's biological father with Bess, or why she had never told me, why she had now brought him to meet me. Was Noah the son I had hoped for? From that day onwards Noah would be seldom out of my mind and the time to find out would come soon enough.

Chapter 47

A year quickly passed. I didn't have the courage to chase Bess. I told myself that I didn't want to disturb Noah's life. I feared rejection and was frightened of upsetting Georgina. I should have known better. Georgina unselfishly wanted whatever I wanted and always supported me as I was to discover on the night of the stock market collapse.

Georgina and I stayed at Claridges Hotel, the beautiful old hotel rebuilt in Brook Street 160 years ago and always regarded as one of London's finest, before an evening at the Royal Opera House. We were going to see Mozart's *The Magic Flute* when news of the stock market crash was announced.

The huge worldwide demands on the insurance companies had led to a massive sell-off of their securities and prices tumbled. Temperature rises, water shortages, drought, and weed and pest invasions had all played a part in slowing economic growth, but the intense storm damage and saltwater invasion had pushed markets into panic. Governments around the world could no longer bail out these massive institutions. We were shocked to see our investments tumble in value, but perhaps this destruction of wealth would calm the growing divide between the super-wealthy and the working man.

Perhaps a new order would emerge where endeavour,

ingenuity and effort would have a true reward rather than the power of capital to create more wealth. The harmony of human society, imagined in the opera, could be restored by the equality Mozart saw achieved by pure love. From penury could come hope.

Although the opera was brilliant, the only interval talk was about the disaster of investment losses, as the wealthy theatregoers ignored the plight of those unfortunate victims of climate change and worried only about their own financial misfortune. Share values would eventually recover, but the sea-swamped farmlands of Norfolk and Suffolk were lost forever, as was much of southern Florida and the seaboard of Louisiana and the Indian coastal cities of Mumbai, Kochi and Chennai. It was a changed world that demanded changed priorities and, yet again, a new normal. It was the New Bird Flu Pandemic that was to finally change the world.

Chapter 48

It is a warm evening now and everything looks perfect for my final dinner. I plan to eat on the veranda. I have not heard from my guest, and I hope I don't have to eat with Peter. Economics seems back to normal now, but after the stock market crash, when we thought that things couldn't get any worse, the country suffered yet another pandemic.

We spent two years frightened to leave our home during the New Bird Flu pandemic that killed almost a third of the population worldwide. The bird flu virus that had been endemic for most of the century mutated into a new virus that transmitted to farm animals, raced through the confined conditions of pig farms and was eventually fatal for human beings.

The virus was dormant in humans for two to three months before symptoms could be detected and then leaving only a short life before the patient's demise. Scientists raced for a cure and a vaccine but to no avail. In the crowded cities, almost half the population succumbed to this easily transmitted disease before it was diagnosed and most of them died.

In the countryside contact with others, and therefore transmission, was much less. Georgina and I stayed at home, frightened to contact anyone and relying on our organic vegetable garden for our food. We kept in touch with our friends through our MediSpecs.

The virus subsided around the world as quickly as it arrived, although no cure or vaccine was ever established. Nations were changed by the reduced populations and the close association with death. Animal factory farming was recognised as the source of disease transmission with such terrible consequences and whatever standards of animal husbandry demanded, none could be sufficient to prevent a further pandemic. The memories of 2020 and 2038 were fuelled by media references.

Georgina and I joined two million people who marched on Westminster demanding an end to animal farming. One of the marchers was Noah and by co-incidence our paths crossed briefly and he acknowledged me with a smile and a wave. Was this compassionate man my son, being a better man than me? Out of adversity came hope.

PART THREE

Realisations

Men generally think me such a foe

To all mankind. Why should I? By them

I lost not what I lost; rather

By them I gained what I gained

Paradise Regained

John Milton 1671

Chapter 49

I am getting tired now. It's hard to focus and it will soon be time for dinner. My guest hasn't arrived. I'm not hungry, but Peter is programmed to serve dinner at 7:30 pm and I've lost the will or memory to record a change. He will switch off automatically at midnight when I must take my euthanasia pill. Perhaps I will be ready by then. My study here has always been my friendly place, a place where I can think, and today is no exception. I am jealous of whoever takes my place. My study has its own patina just like the once crumbling enduring Parliament buildings.

I was in the Stranger's Gallery at the House of Commons to hear the passing of the legislation that would finally bring an end to factory farming and eventually to a ban on all animal farming.

Conservative Prime Minister William Shaft had to respond to the public outcry against animal farming despite his agricultural backers and ban the production and import of animal products by restraining animals indoors. This would have massive ramifications throughout the farming community and lead in turn to riots and freedom demands by farmers and right-wing anarchist groups, but, at last, it was not unusual to be vegan. It was now only the fringe of society that was still eating meat, fish or dairy products.

President Hank Brennan in the United States quickly

followed suit, urged on by past President Jane Willis, who had herself fought for this outcome on ethical grounds. President Brennan took advantage of the popular feelings to bring about legislation that would ease major pollution and water shortages, brought about by the expansion of mega-farms earlier in the century.

The new bill didn't restrict beef production. This would only come later when Americans became aware of how their beef-eating tradition was seen as barbarism by the rest of the developed world.

Similar legislation was passed in the EU, many African countries, and India. All factory farms in China were closed at the beginning of the New Bird Flu pandemic and would never reopen.

Russia was slower to react, but all the new agricultural land in the warming climate of Siberia was devoted to plant production for human consumption and demand for animal products rapidly declined due to cost and availability.

At last mid-century hope was being reflected by late-century government response.

COP74 October 2068 London England

COP74 was held in London. Delegates were invited to attend. World temperatures had held at 2.1 degrees above pre-industrial levels. Sea levels continued to rise and were now 90cm above the level in 2000. The bird flu pandemic of seven years ago caused an unwanted fall in the world population to 7.5 billion. A reduction in animal farming, fossil fuel control and carbon capture had reduced greenhouse gases. The collapse of the fishing industry allowed some ocean recovery.

Chapter 50

I don't like thinking of funerals, especially now, but I must mention my mother's. It was a quiet affair. She had accepted the euthanasia policy. The frail old lady that my mother had become had enjoyed extremely good health after her breast cancer cure but had now reached a time when life held little promise for her. Many of her friends had already succumbed to the inevitable, mostly from natural causes but sometimes with the same euthanasia pill that would end my mother's life.

I had always taken my mother for granted. Maybe because I had no children of my own, or so I thought. It was only now that I stopped to remember all the sacrifices she had made for me, and my two sisters. She had been a young woman when I was born, with a career in journalism brought to a premature end by childbirth.

After her three children left home, she felt middle-aged and unwanted in a society that still valued youth and beauty above experience and passion. Her freelance work had found an audience amongst social media magazines but enthusiasm for reading informative articles had already waned by the time she returned to the workplace. She then wrote technical leaflets for a software house before retiring when they realised that she misunderstood youthful jargon. I had done little to repay the support she always gave me, and, whilst I valued the freedom she had shown me, I now regretted that

I had not shown her the love and respect she so richly deserved.

The harshness of the Government's euthanasia policy, which I had encouraged all those years ago, struck me hard. Although my mother had never really been happy since the death of my father 20 years ago and was ready to complete her life with dignity, I felt suddenly lonely. Having a living parent is a comfort I had not understood until she died. Although I had expected her passing for each of the last ten years as we awaited the medical health assessment, I was not ready for this condemning result. Society had benefited generally from this policy with a more efficient health service, but I didn't feel the price was acceptable when my family faced saying goodbye.

Chapter 51

An evening glass of sherry or a gin and tonic remains the pre-dinner drink of choice for most people, but I prefer the bitter taste of whisky to prepare my palate. I have some Macallan single malt that I put down many years ago. Goodness knows what it's worth now, but that doesn't matter to me.

Peter has brought me a small glass of the golden liquid. Etiquette demands that I don't start before my guest arrives but I'm giving up hope of that. Perhaps I wouldn't be expecting anybody at all if I hadn't visited the London Olympics in 2072.

Georgina and I visited the London Olympics for finals day. By coincidence, I met Bess. I allowed my curiosity to outweigh my caution and ask her about Noah.

The Olympics had returned to London after sixty years, but it no longer attracted the 10 million spectators of the early part of the century. An enthusiastic crowd enjoyed the intense competition and the UK came third in the overall table of medal winners, mostly as a result of the five gold medals won by Chester White in the computer gaming arena.

A falling world population had slowed world economies and reduced prosperity whilst high-cost air travel was less popular, reducing the attending audiences. The creation of new sporting records had declined and no running records had been recorded for eight years, as the development of strength and speed in the human body appeared to have reached a pinnacle. The Olympic events were broadcast worldwide but even media audiences continued to decline.

It was a coincidence that Bess was also at the event and even more unlikely that we should meet. It was at the refreshment bar that I spotted her with a group of her girlfriends, enjoying a glass of wine and a break from the heat of the day. She seemed happy to see me, and I asked the question that had been on my lips now for several years.

"Is Noah my son?"

"No, he is my son," was her flustered reply.

"Yes, but am I his father?"

It was then that, unexpectedly, Bess broke into floods of tears. Her friends rushed to her side, wondering what I had done or said. She brushed them aside with a wave of her arm and a relieved smile that averted a scene.

"Yes," Bess said. "Luke, you are Noah's father. I've kept it secret for nearly sixty years."

"Does he know?"

"No, even he doesn't know, but now I must tell him".

Can I see him?"

Chapter 52

I think that Bess told Noah that I was his father, but he had declined to see me. She never said so outright, but there was always a reason why we couldn't meet. I hoped that he would come to my seventieth birthday party, but he showed no signs of a change of heart and Georgina and I decided that we would have a holiday abroad.

We had not been able to afford travel much since the collapse of our share portfolio ten years ago, but my book sales had enjoyed a resurgence as readers wondered at the madness of the early century now that the world's society was finding more harmony. We found an old holiday brochure and were amazed at the number of places that had disappeared under the sea. Of course, Jakarta had sunk below the sea almost 35 years ago, but it had been followed by all of the Bahama Islands, including Grand Bahama and the capital, Nassau.

Panama City and Tabasco in Mexico, Bangkok in Thailand and Ho Chi Minh City in Vietnam were all places we could no longer visit. Nearer to home Bruges in Belgium, Delft in the Netherlands and Ribe in Denmark were now underwater. Of course, the coastal towns of Italy, Greece, Spain and Portugal could not be saved and many of the treasures of the Roman, Christian, Byzantine and Venetian civilisations were lost with them. In the UK, Norfolk and Suffolk in east England had almost disappeared under the sea as the fens had been flooded.

Falling inland water levels, regular landslides and agricultural pollution had all but destroyed the Lake District in the northwest. Rising sea levels and coastal erosion had substantially reduced the land mass of the Principality of Wales. Everywhere from the Caribbean to Southport, from Blackpool to Newquay, the shallow beaches had been lost, and tourism had been hit by their disappearance as rising sea levels reached coastal development. Unsettled political disputes over scarce water supplies were still causing conflict in Africa following the drying of Lake Chad. The uncertainty about tourist safety further reduced our travel options.

Coastal areas of Japan had disappeared despite massive investment in sea wall protection. The Philippines had been abandoned as upland grasslands had suffered devastating fires each summer's drought in the last decade whilst there were water shortages in spite of the increased frequency of torrential rain storms. Sea level rises combined with the sinking cities as the water table was destroyed, making the towns and cities untenable.

Over 100 million people had been relocated after the eruption of Mount Pinatubo in the Philippines in an international deal that brought workers to the growing northern countries of Russia and Canada. This process created a huge surge in the value of the rouble and halted the decline of the dollar.

The Seychelles were also uninhabited as rising sea levels had left only a few of the tallest mountains above sea level. The hundred thousand human inhabitants and the abundant wildlife had not been so lucky. As the warming polluted seas denied them the traditional creole fish diet, and failed crops from extreme temperatures prevented the growing of foods, the poor people of the archipelago could not survive. Many died of starvation as the rest of the world wrestled with their own problems. A similar story was experienced in the coral islands of the Maldives, where the islands had disappeared and, with them any tourist trade that had fuelled the economy.

In the three hundred islands of Fiji in the South Pacific, off the east of Australia, a massive relocation plan started early in the century had moved one hundred and forty-two coastal villages inland and to higher ground to avoid rising sea levels. Many of the relieved communities were by now again in villages on the new coastline and with their old way of life protected. The ever-present prospect of tropical cyclones and the unbearable summer heat made Fiji another destination that was now unsuitable for a holiday.

Memories of a different planet only increased Georgina's depression and, after lots of talking, we decided that walking in the Alps would clear our minds and remind us that this planet still had beauty spots. And what a beauty spot it was when we arrived at Le Grand Bellevue in Gstaad, Switzerland. The hotel is a fairy-tale turreted palace set in a private manicured parkland in the middle of the elegant village of Gstaad.

The hotel was first opened in 1912 and the English country-style architecture and fittings had been maintained to provide a comfortable ambience to help Georgina recover from her memories of Nigeria. Originally a nearly all-year-round ski resort, Gstaad had re-invented itself as a place of relaxation and walking when the glacier 3000 had melted. The Grand Bellevue boasted the largest Spa in the village.

Maybe those wretched candles played a part, but Georgina and I felt out of place despite the opulence and beauty. Although I was over seventy and Georgina not far behind, we were not yet ready for the idle life of the lazy rich, although we did enjoy Leonards, the Michelin-star restaurant in the hotel. We spent our days together exploring the many country trails over the beautiful mountains.

The beauty of the Alps only reminded Georgina of the contrast with her experiences in Nigeria. Her feeling of guilt that our pleasures were still denied to so many others made her more aware of the increasing deprivation others suffered. Her kindness of thought was inspiring, but her melancholy was a burden that we would both carry.

Georgina's feeling of hopelessness was matched by angry outbursts over small matters, insomnia and a lack of interest in almost everything. Georgina's life reflected her frustration that the world government had allowed such pain to so many.

Capitalist ideologies have enabled short-term strategies in the pursuit of wealth to ignore the longer-term needs of the planet. Outcomes that were predicted in the twentieth century could have been averted by action then and in the early part of this century. Inaction, international big business interest and electoral necessity had obstructed change, and we all carried responsibility.

Chapter 53

The Palace announced the death of King William V who had escaped the euthanasia pill for 12 years but was now in such poor health that his Royal connections could no longer protect him from the law of the country. I wasn't in London for the funeral of King William V or the Coronation of King George, his 62-year-old son, who had proved to be such a disappointment. His early interest in the Planet for Pleasure had given him environmental credentials but had not changed his personal indulgent lifestyle.

King George VII restored the splendour and pageantry of earlier years even though such pomp and ceremony were distasteful in modern society. I doubted that the over-indulged King George could ever be a popular Head of State.

I knew then that the Monarchy could not survive. The obese incumbent with his beautiful wife and obvious mistresses could not be seen as a representative of our country in a society that valued appearance before all else.

The trend for physical perfection with the surgeon's knife had begun early in the century. Now, with more time and money amongst many of us, as AI fulfilled more and more business roles, the demand for perceived physical perfection has grown exponentially. But not as far as King George VII. I imagine his position left him with nobody to impress and his liking for claret seemed to be part of his heritage. King William and Queen Kate must regret naming their firstborn son after a line of Georges that included the mad King

George III and the profligate squanderer, his son George IV. It will be many years before my expectations of an elected Head of State will be fulfilled.

COP84 Paris France October 2074

COP 84, held in Paris, was the final Climate Conference, fittingly held where it had all started with the Paris Agreement of 2015.

The world temperature was held at 2.1 degrees above pre-industrial levels. Sea levels had risen to 110cm above 2000 levels and would continue to rise.

Many islands and lowland areas had been totally lost to the seas. Countries close to the equator were too hot for life. Ice melt and the release of the permafrost was continuing. The world population had grown to eight billion.

Tree planting and re-wilding had restored the equivalent of the Amazon rainforest. The restoration of natural habitat had halted species decline. Extreme weather events had settled into a new pattern. Animal agriculture has been banned in the UK, US, EU and Australia.

Vegetables were grown on efficient vertical farms. Scientists were predicting that world temperatures would decline during the 22nd century. Rising sea levels would continue but an increase of 1.5 metres in the sea level was considered the maximum.

Climate change had been a worldwide catastrophe but the planet was adapting and human animals would survive.

Chapter 54

My hoped-for visitor has still not arrived. It's getting late and I'm feeling a bit down. I'll ask Peter for another glass of malt whisky. Whilst he is fetching it, I will turn my mind to a happier time.

Georgina and I rented a cottage in the village of Baslow, close to the famous Chatsworth House, the country seat of 17 generations of the Dukes of Devonshire, where the annual country fair was being held. The gardens at Chatsworth had been largely unchanged for 500 years but now the warming climate and water shortages had required major modification.

The famous 19th Century Emperor Fountain, built for the expected visit of Tsar Nicholas I in 1843 by the sixth Duke, remained unused as the feed lake had dried in the summer drought. The once pristine lawn was replaced by browning, unruly meadowland and the thousand-acre parkland surrounding the house had been re-wilded more than 20 years ago as part of the Prince of Wales Planet for Pleasure Initiative. By planting native trees capable of withstanding the climate extremes, such as holm oak, red maple and golden willow and introducing cattle and boars to break up the ground, wild flora had taken root and wildlife had returned.

The ground was covered with wildflowers as white daisies

and colourful zinnias fought for space against the golden dandelion. We saw a woodpecker, a peregrine falcon, butterflies, bees and evidence of beavers as we walked the grounds.

Chatsworth House continued to display the masterpieces of art and sculpture collected by generations of Dukes and Duchesses and there was something very moving about seeing the original paintings by Rembrandt, Reynolds and Veronese. We had exact replicas available through AI oil painting, but they did not carry the same emotional connection.

The centre of Baslow was little changed over the years and St Anne's Church, the Prince of Wales pub and the local cricket square remained the focus of activity. Beyond the village centre, fields developed with Jaguar Land Rover eco homes were still largely empty. This was a stark expression of the changes we had experienced.

As nature thrived the human species had declined through the New Bird Flu Pandemic, creating hope for the planet and those of us who had survived at the cost of so many deaths. It was reminiscent of the nearby village of Eyam, where the Black Death of the late seventeenth century had been contained by the villagers' isolation but at a terrible cost to the population.

Chapter 55

The whisky has arrived and I will need it if I am to recount my darkest moments without a silly burst of tears. I cry for Georgina, for all she gave and all she missed. I cry for Bess, mother of the son I may never know. I cry for all my friends. Most have passed. It is natural to want to live, but I wonder why I remain when so many have gone. It's getting late. I am tired. My wanted guest has not arrived. I want to feel despondent as I tell you about Georgina.

It was a very normal morning that would turn into my worst nightmare. Georgina and I woke quite late as the darkness was slow to move on this damp January morning. Lying in bed, Georgina and I fondly held hands and discussed our day's plans as we did on most mornings. I suggested maybe we could have tea in bed as we were not in a hurry to start the day. Georgina complained of a headache but went downstairs to make the tea. When I followed her half an hour later to question the delay, I found my wife had collapsed on the floor. The ambulance was quick to arrive but not quick enough. Georgina had died at the age of 69. She was at last released from the agonising frustration and depression that had haunted her since her visit to Nigeria almost thirty years earlier. I was devastated. A cerebral aneurysm had taken her from me in a second. Georgina had been my constant companion, my only real confidant, and my abiding encouragement from the very moment we met after the

Ariana Grande concert in 2046. Georgina had many guests at her funeral and her many work colleagues praised her commitment to improving the planet's kindness. I was too broken to hear or notice. The candles had finally spluttered to their end. Now I was on my own.

My life had to continue, and my time was spent in quiet and often lonely contemplation for several weeks. I turned to my oldest friends for companionship and spent my time still regularly exercising, doing lots of reading and continuing with my rather hopeless attempts to manoeuvre a small white ball into an eleven centimetres diameter hole inconveniently placed too many metres away on the golf course. It was on the golf course that I met Jacob Williams.

Chapter 56

I always smile when I think of Jacob, and I need a smile and another taste of my favourite whisky. Jacob would have been ready to share the bottle with me. He passed only two years ago. My best friend since Georgina died and a kind thoughtful man, if sometimes rather headstrong. His trademark bow tie when it was no longer fashionable made him memorable, but it was because he was so easy to like that our charity attracted such support.

Jacob had been a good golfer, but age had brought a decline and widowhood that we both shared. He didn't want to discuss his past but gradually, I discovered that he had been an early manufacturer of plant-based dog food and his brand had captured a growing market nearly sixty years ago. Dogs were eating 20% of the meat consumed in the UK back in the early part of the century and consumers had been slow to recognise the huge environmental cost. The concept of killing one animal to feed another did not seem strange when I was a boy.

Whilst the Kennel Club had been heavily sponsored by the major meat and fish-based dog food companies it had propagated the notion that meat and fish were an essential part of a canine diet. Indeed, some owners had been threatened with legal action for cruelty to their pets when they denied their dogs meat. Slowly evidence blew the myth and, as meat and fish products became more expensive, they became less desired. Jacob's business, Plant Pot Dog Food, had flourished. When the major producers fully entered the plant-based dog food market, his business was well-placed to compete. He had recently taken advantage of a newly buoyant stock market to sell his business for many millions of pounds.

With no surviving heirs, Jacob was determined to spend it whilst he could see the benefit of his altruism. He invited me to join the Board of his charity. I, too, had no heirs, a substantial share portfolio of my own, a small but helpful income from continuing book sales and some connections around the world. I sold my Stephanie Lane original artwork, bought all those years ago in Berlin, for a staggering thirteen million pounds and invested it all and most of my share portfolio in the charity. I was delighted to join forces with Jacob and together we would try to use our money and our connections to do some good.

There were many demanding claims as the world adapted to the changes brought about by rising temperatures. Jacob and I decided to invest in businesses that could use the new world climate to provide work and fulfilment to society. In the UK, we supported the Duke of Wales's Planet for Pleasure Initiative re-wilding projects that provided public open spaces and habitat for wildlife and the retained farm animals. We only supported operations that allowed animal populations to be self-regulating and gave dead creatures a quiet burial. There is no excuse for animal abuse.

In India, Bangladesh and Pakistan, we established a fund to pay the costs of moving families from flood-stricken areas to places of safety. The charity negotiated group visas to allow working citizens to resettle in countries needing to increase the workforce where we could provide for communities to move together to maintain the connections and support essential for their happy life.

Anastas, the personable young man who had shown me around Moscow 35 years ago, had become a leading Russian politician until his retirement only five years earlier. He had inherited his father's vast fortune and was ready to use it for the common good. After a successful career as a hotelier, he had been an elected member of The Federation Council of the Russian Federation for over twenty-five years. With his advice, connections and part of his father's land sale wealth, we were able to buy agriculture machinery to fund organic farming in the newly fertile steppes in Siberia, but only where they employed migrants from the devastated lands of India, Bangladesh and Pakistan. Alongside the agricultural support, we invested in the lithium mines in the area, with the Russian government and Anastas 's support.

In Israel, I enlisted the help of Jessica, the still beautiful dairy-free milk producer I had met and very briefly loved fifty years ago. Jessica had never married, and had no dependent heirs and she, too, welcomed the opportunity to align her resources with our charitable ambition. With her guidance, some of her vast fortune and the ingenuity of her fellow countrymen and women, we designed and built the new superpower storage system that now fuels our homes using lithium-ion mined in the newly warmed area of Siberia.

I am most proud of our work in Barnaul a once beautiful city built on the western banks of the River Ob, in the southwest of Siberia. We used the charity to starter-fund a huge building programme to house the many new immigrants that quickly tripled the population to two million inhabitants. Extreme cold in the winter months had prevented construction until new methods of building, a warming climate and my connection with the Jaguar Land Rover house production enabled year-round working.

The new influx of workers allowed a continuous programme of restoration for the fine 18th and 19th Century civic halls built from the wealth of the copper mines. The improving climate made life in Barnaul almost viable, although summer temperatures made air cooling essential. I visited often in the Spring and Autumn months as I watched our investments take shape and enjoyed strolling around the park and the pine forests in the constant sunshine. I experienced the sense of pride in the community that our spending had engendered and that had enabled the influx of migrant labour without trouble.

I felt a special connection with Nigeria and, in Georgina's memory, we embraced a massive birth control advertising promotion alongside a residential building programme in conjunction with Jaguar Land Rover.

These charitable works provided a focus for me and an excuse for travel as I helped choose and supervise our projects. We invested to make the world a better place, but our investments generally provided a growing profit that we then re-invested. Jacob and I were getting older and my search for successors for the charity took many months until we decided to hand it over to youth. We selected a new board of enthusiasts under 30, believing that the confidence of the young trumps experience. I have watched their success.

Wherever I went throughout the world, I observed a new kindness as the aspirations of President Jackson Hendrix James, expressed so many years ago, came to fruition. A quieter planet without the petrol combustion engine, a more compassionate world without animal slaughter, and a more peaceful world without competition for territory was making the kinder place that Jackson and I had discussed in Washington when I was still a university student.

Following the Bird Flu Pandemic, there had been a boom in childbirth and populations were growing back. With learning facts no longer required, because of the wealth of knowledge available via Meta K, schooling was able to focus on how we should live together with empathy and compassion and share the planet's resources.

Children are better educated in the habitat of the many creatures that share our planet. The open re-wilded spaces helped foster our understanding of fellow earthlings. The growth in technology has changed the concept of both learning and work. Secularism has diminished differences and conflict and allowed tolerance of varying views.

Chapter 57

I've just started my third glass of this fine fifty-five-year-old Macallan Malt. At least I don't have to worry about a hangover in the morning. It no longer matters if it affects the heart condition that rendered me ready for the euthanasia pill.

When I wrote this book, *The Future Past of an Extraordinary Man*, now more than forty years ago, I had to imagine the loneliness and anonymity of my old age. Now I realise dying is not as frightening as the young me thought.

As I meander towards the end of my story, I am starting to feel ready for that inevitable pill. Throughout my life, I have held an interest in politics, but it was only because of my charity work that I was able to see the inner workings of the Houses of Parliament.

Lord Shaft of Shaftesbury invited Jacob and me to lunch with him in the Houses of Parliament. Jacob had been trying to persuade the Ex-Prime Minister to support our charity and he had requested a meeting. We were happy to attend and although, in the end, it proved fruitless as a fundraising exercise, it was a special occasion.

The buildings had almost completed a total refurbishment at a cost of almost £30 billion. Inside they were restored to their Victorian Gothic style and probably looked their best since the re-constructed Palace of Westminster was finished in

1870. I hoped for a private tour of the building but it wasn't to be.

Once our security clearance had been checked, we were accompanied by a guide to one of the many small private dining rooms. The standard of food was ordinary, but the company was lively and full of political gossip. William Shaft entertained Jacob and me with three of his contemporary colleagues in these historic surroundings, making the House of Lords still the best club in London.

As the Ex-Members of Parliament reminisced about their time in office, I asked what they thought was the major change to society during the 21st Century. I expected the change in eating habits that was improving health and having a very positive impact on climate change, pollution and the vibrancy of nature, to be at the top of their list. In that, I was mistaken.

All our fellow guests declared that the use of Facial Recognition Technology was the industrial revolution of the century, as important as the internet in the 20th Century, mechanisation in the 18th and 19th Centuries and the printing press in the 15th Century. They reminded us that at the beginning of the 21st Century, people used paper notes or plastic cards to make payments, carried paper and card travel documents, started their homes and vehicles with keys and signed a form to vote.

Despite Civil Liberty campaigns, Facial Recognition

Technology has been slowly introduced into all our lives. We now shopped by collecting items from the store, restaurant or bar without thinking of payment as it was all registered against our account by facial recognition. It was a criminal offence to spend beyond your agreed limit and criminal prosecution and a substantial fine were automatic. Our income was registered to our account and our taxes were calculated from our income and expenditure records, any liability charged to our account. The technology has almost totally prevented tax fraud and identity theft. The Burglary had declined because there was no cash to steal and no mechanism for the sale of stolen goods. Voter fraud is a thing of the past.

Facial Recognition Technology and the consolidation of records were used for much wider purposes than for money transactions. The consolidation of records made access to personal data easier for the State but ensured to recognition of crime and the location of criminals. Social security payments always found the correct beneficiary and court financial awards were always charged and recovered.

Medical records automatically triggered benefit payments. Vehicles would not start unless by an authorised driver who had a licence and insurance. Removing Passports speeded up border control and illuminated illegal immigration. The paperless society was cheaper to operate, more efficient and less damaging to the environment.

I'd hardly noticed the erosion of personal liberties. As a law-abiding citizen, I had welcomed the changes as they had gradually been introduced, and most had little or no personal impact. I could however see how this concentration of information gave the State great control and influence, and I worry for the future.

Chapter 58

It seems only yesterday that I was celebrating my eightieth birthday with a sense of relief. Despite rather high blood pressure, I passed my medical and toasted the result with champagne.

My eightieth birthday celebration was a quiet affair. Passing my medical promised at least another year of my charitable work, although I was increasingly feeling out of touch with modern thinking. I realised that the young board members looked upon me as being unaware of the needs of the day. Maybe they were right, but at least I believed they liked and respected me. I was there to encourage, not criticise, to support, not demoralise, to advise, not demand. I enjoyed the role.

I met Mia for lunch in London and we reminisced about the lifetime changes we had seen. Her wife, Nova, had passed naturally some fifteen years earlier. I remember her quiet funeral and the eulogy delivered by her brother that captured her life of graceful style and elegant living. We toasted "absent friends" with tears in our eyes as we remembered happy times, past partners and our younger selves. I still mourned Georgina's passing and was feeling a little lonely and sorry for myself until Mia cheered me up with the help of a couple of pills.

In November, it was warm in London. The tree-lined roads

and parklands made London such a beautiful city, with the retained architecture of the 18th and 19th Centuries reminding us of a grander past. The Thames side sea barriers are a stunning example of the modern, brutal style of sleek protection. Tower blocks of office space erected in the late 20th century were converted into homes and vertical farms now that all clerical work was completed by Artificial Intelligence, supervised remotely from the operators' homes.

A falling city population had allowed the clearing of many of the 20th-century slums to make way for new parkland. The collapse of consumerism had allowed a less hurried society, whilst the universal acceptance of plant-based consumption had created a population less accepting of violence towards each other as well as towards animals.

It was hard to imagine that at the beginning of the century, most people were eating the animals we now respected as companions, fellow beings, and other earthlings. It's not so strange when you remember that at the beginning of the century, it was common for doctors to cut open human bodies to cut out disease. 2083 society still wasn't exactly the Utopia described by Thomas More in 1516, but it was moving towards the stability and equality needed for a fair society with nature at the centre.

Mia died three days later, leaving me feeling more and more isolated.

Chapter 59

The day is coming to an end. My final dinner will be a lonely affair, as has been much of my life since Georgina passed. My final memory will be recording these events in my life, some remembered clearly, some perhaps re-imagined and maybe some inflated by time and a declining brain.

The memories have made me both proud and ashamed. They are my memories of a life lived and the human experience unique to each of us, a reminder that nobody is ordinary. Everyone is extraordinary in their own way.

Years have passed when I have quietly handed over to others to pursue their ambitions for change, safe in the knowledge that our species will always find a way to adapt to the challenges of life.

I don't want to die. I am curious about the future of human life on our changing planet. Will President Devin's party and the USA continue to dominate world culture, or will China's purchase of influence throughout the planet determine the cultural and political future? Will the Russian Imperial ambition return? Will the cheap labour in newly industrialised Africa give that continent a stronger role in the future? Will the message of animal freedoms, now so ingrained in Western culture, ever spread to China and Russia? Will the flourishing tree-lined roads of our cities and the abundance of wild parkland succeed in capturing the inevitable carbon pollution of a growing population? Will kindness overcome hate, hope succeed over fear and the natural world restore itself for the benefit of us all?

I think that I can hear Peter letting somebody in through the front door.

MetaNews. 29 November 2091

It is with great sadness that we report the passing of Luke Macdonald, the well-known philanthropist. Mr. Macdonald died peacefully of a heart attack at his home in Surrey. He was accompanied by his only son, the crime writer Noah Hurley.

The charity Mr. Macdonald founded with his partner, Jacob Williams, has donated over four billion pounds to resettlement projects throughout the world. The funeral is to be held in Westminster Abbey on the 9 December. No flowers; his casket will be adorned by four red candles. It is expected to be attended by his many friends.

Acknowledgements

Many people have helped me with this book, and I would like to thank all the many scientists and campaigners who have recognized the dangers of man induced climate change and the contribution made by our food chain. My optimism for the future is entirely dependent on their messages being heard, understood and acted upon.

My daughter, the author Sarah Clarke, has been unstinting in her support and advice, and my wife Susan's impatience for change has driven me forward. My special thanks go to them.

Without the contribution of my editor, Sally OJ and the team at Amazon, I could not have brought my ideas to the page.

Printed in Great Britain
by Amazon

59407756R00159